Love Begins in Winter

Also by Simon Van Booy

The Secret Lives of People in Love

Love Begins in Winter

FIVE STORIES

Simon Van Booy

HARPER PERENNIAL

NEW YORK ● LONDON ● TORONTO ● SYDNEY ● NEW DELHI ● AUCKLAND

HARPER ● PERENNIAL

FIRST EDITION

Designed by Jamie Kerner

Library of Congress Cataloging-in-Publication Data is available upon request.

ISBN 978-0-06-166147-1

09   10   11   12   13   OV/RRD   10   9   8   7   6   5   4   3   2   1

to

LORILEE VAN BOOY

If you are not here, then why are you everywhere?

Contents

Love Begins in Winter

I

I WAIT IN THE SHADOWS.

My cello is already on stage. It was carved in 1723 on a Sicilian hillside where the sea is very quiet. The strings vibrate when the bow is near, as though anticipating their lover.

My name is Bruno Bonnet. The curtain I stand behind is the color of a plum. The velvet is heavy. My life is on the other side. Sometimes I wish it would continue on without me.

The stage lights here in Quebec City are too bright. Stars of dust circle the scroll and the pegs as I am introduced in French-Canadian. The cello belonged to my grandfather who was accidentally killed in World War II.

My grandfather's kitchen chair is also on stage. I can only put weight on three legs. The wicker at the center of the seat is ripped. One day it's going to collapse. When the chair arrives at the concert hall a day or so before a performance, a frantic music director will call with bad news: "Your chair has been utterly ruined in transit."

An eruption of applause and I take the stage.

Who are all these people?

One day I will play without my instrument. I will sit up straight and not move. I will close my eyes and imagine life taking place in the houses outside the concert hall: steaming pots stirred by women in slippers; teenagers in their rooms wearing headphones; somebody's son looking for his keys; a divorcée brushing her teeth as her cat stares; a family watching television—the youngest is asleep but will not remember his dream.

When I clasp my bow, the audience is suddenly very quiet.

I look out at their faces a moment before I begin.

So many people and yet not one single person who knows anything about me.

If only one of them recognized me, I could slip from the branches of my life, brush time from my clothes, and begin the long journey across the fields to the place where I first disappeared. A boy leaning crookedly on a gate, waiting for his best friend to get up. The back wheel of Anna's bicycle still spinning.

For ten years as a professional cellist I have been raising the dead in concert halls across the world. The moment my bow makes contact with the strings, Anna's form appears. She is wearing the clothes from that day. I am twenty years older. But she is still a child. She flickers because she is made of light. She watches a few feet from my cello. She looks at me but doesn't recognize who I am.

Tonight the concert hall is packed. By the end of the final movement I can sense her fading. Perhaps a single hand remains; a scoop of shoulder; a shimmering mane of hair.

But she is turning inward quickly now—quickly drifting from the living world.

Some concert performers turn their backs to the figures that float upon the stage: figures that move with the confusion of sleep, with the grace of unfurling smoke, figures conjured by guilt, love, regret, luck, and happenstance. Some performers I've read about can't take their eyes off them. Some crack and fling themselves off bridges; others drink themselves into oblivion or stand in freezing rivers at midnight.

I think music is what language once aspired to be. Music allows us to face God on our own terms because it reaches beyond life.

I feel moments from the end.

The muscles in my bowing arm tighten. The final notes are sonorous; I steady my bow like an oar held in a river, steering us all toward the bank of now and tomorrow and the day after that. Days ahead like open fields.

And night pools outside the concert hall. The city is still wet. The concert hall is glassed in and overlooks a garden. Eyes of rain dot the windows and shiver with each breath of wind. Stars fill the sky, then drop to flood the streets and the squares. When it rains, even the most insignificant puddle is a map of the universe.

When the performance ends, I stand and raise my bow to the audience. I can hear things landing on the stage—flowers and small letters taped to the plastic.

The applause is deafening. I feel for Anna's mitten in my pocket.

I drip with sweat under the lights. Each drop holds its own tiny clapping audience. As always I want something sweet to drink. I hurry off the stage, still holding my bow. When I reach the steps, I feel again for Anna's mitten and suddenly see her face with terrifying clarity. Such straight hair and so many freckles. The only authentic memories find us—like letters addressed to someone we used to be.

I hurry to my dressing room. I find a towel, drink orange juice from a bottle, and fall into a chair.

Then I sit very still and close my eyes.

Another concert over.

I wonder how many more I can do. How many Annas are left. She was twelve when she died. Her father was a baker—and since that morning, every twelfth baguette he bakes bears the letter A. He lets children eat cakes in his shop for free. They talk loudly and make a mess.

A porter knocks, then enters my dressing room with a cell phone. He gestures for me to take it. He has the sort of square shoulders women like. There are deep lines around his eyes, but he doesn't look over forty. I give him my bottle of juice. He holds it at a distance from his body. I cup the phone to my ear. It's Sandy. She wants to know how it has gone. She couldn't hear because of the static on the porter's phone. Someone had given her the number so she could listen from backstage. Sandy is my agent. She is originally from Iowa. A good businesswoman; understands how creative minds work—in other words, she's pushy with everyone but her talent. I tell her it went well. Then I ask if I can tell her something.

"Like what?" she says.

I seldom volunteer anything. For most of my thirties, I have seen little point in telling people anything. But as a teenager, I loved passionately, spent whole nights crying (for what, I can no longer remember). I followed women home and then wrote sonatas that I left on doorsteps in the middle of the night. I dived into ponds fully clothed. I almost drank myself to death. In my youth, all conflict was resolution—just a busier form of emptiness.

Sandy knows only that I'm French and that I never forget to send her daughter a postcard from wherever I go.

I tell Sandy about a dream I had on the flight to Quebec City. Sandy says that dreams are either unresolved conflicts or wish fulfillments. According to Freud, she says. Then she doesn't say anything. I can hear a television in the background. Then she says her daughter needs to go to bed. I ask what she's done wrong. Sandy laughs. They are knitting and there's a film on. Sandy is a single mother. She went to a facility and had herself impregnated. I've always thought that if Sandy died, I'd want her daughter to live with me. I could teach her the cello. Though she'd be alone a lot because I go away.

Still, I would leave her "notes" all over the house. We could name the two eighteenth-century portraits that hang in my apartment. They could watch over us. We could watch over each other.

I give the porter his telephone back and thank him. He asks if it is good news.

My plane is not leaving for New York until the next afternoon. I have an entire evening to wander around. I arrived in Quebec City just this morning. The taxi driver was from Bosnia. He wore a wool hat with the symbol of his favorite football team.

About half an hour after my performance at the Musée de la Civilisation ended, several couples flooded my dressing room and invited me to dinner. These couples are the same in every city. In the ancient Sicilian town of Noto (where my cello was made), their garments would have borne the most intricate patterns. I imagine faces, people sitting in courtyards: the luxury of shade; lips wet with wine; dusty feet resting atop sandals; the smell of horses from outside; children running through the house, curls bouncing off shoulders; laughter turns to crying—the scope of human feeling hasn't changed.

I'm always asked to dinner or to spend the weekend somewhere with the trustees—perhaps I might even bring my cello? they ask.

When I was young, I was too shy to refuse. For the past several years, I've politely declined. Sandy says I'm getting a reputation for being difficult.

I explained like always that I must recover; that I have been hampered by a rather serious cold. I took a few deep breaths for effect. A woman laughed. Her husband put his arm around her. He was wearing a canary-yellow bow tie. There were dark patches under his eyes.

Before the performance I looked at myself in the mirror. I wondered if I should shave. It was my birthday last Wednesday, and I have thirty-five years attached to me like a belt of weights. Actually, years mean nothing. It's what's inside them. To some I am a famous cellist. Bruno Bonnet. I don't know what I am to myself, probably still a scared little boy enchanted by the world, or, at best, the boy whose face has remained glued to the misty back window of the family sedan, a brown Renault 16. As a child, my family would take long drives, often not even stopping for the night. I think my father drove the way he thought. My mother would break bread and give my brother and me handfuls each. When the bread was gone, we would finally stop. Bread was the civilizing force of my childhood.

My father was one of the few men I knew growing up who didn't smoke. His father was killed in the war. As Paris filled up with Nazi soldiers shouting and pointing things out, the roads south were clogged with people—their possessions loaded onto cars, horse-drawn wagons, baby carriages loaded with radios, family pictures, and cutlery. Hitler wanted the roads destroyed.

It wasn't difficult for the pilots of the Luftwaffe to spot the roads from above because they were literally moving. My grandfather was plowing a field. His head was clipped by a piece of shell. My father was ten.

When I was ten, my father gave me a photograph of his father holding his ancient Italian cello. He told me to save it, that one day it would mean something. I remember telling him that it already meant something. Then I asked casually if I could learn the cello. I wasn't aware of what I'd said.

A few weeks later on Christmas Eve, there was a priceless eighteenth-century cello sitting under the tree. It was my grandfather's; the case bore his initials. My mother had tied a ribbon around the case. As I approached it, my father got up and left the room.

My father listened to me practice with tears in his eyes. That's the secret to my success as a cellist.

As my dressing room gradually emptied, the man with the canary-yellow bow tie asked if he and his wife could take my cello in their car to my hotel, the Chateau Frontenac, where they planned to dine at Jean Souchard's restaurant. His wife said they would be more careful than I could imagine. I thanked them and explained how the music director had already arranged for the cello to be escorted to the hotel "vault" by several members of the museum staff. The couple looked disappointed, and so I walked them to their car. They seemed to want something from me. I wanted to explain that trusting is harder than being trusted.

I love walking. Especially when I have nothing to carry (which is not often). On my way back to the hotel it starts to rain, lightly at first, and then hard, half-frozen drops. On the street that leads to the Chateau Frontenac, I stop walking. The road surface is slick. It reflects the world with a beautiful inaccuracy.

My old geography professor once told his class how the music, paintings, sculptures, and books of the world are mirrors in which people see versions of themselves.

There is something about the rain slipping down the hill that prevents me from moving. People hurry past, going somewhere but nowhere. Cars slow down. The people inside want to see what I am looking at. The sweeping whites of the headlights like strange animals.

When I get back to New York, I'm going to memorize the opening lines of Dante's most famous work. I think it begins, "Midway on our life's journey, I found myself in dark woods . . ."

I think of Horowitz's Träumerei. Twenty-five seconds longer than anyone else's. Or did I imagine that? If you haven't heard this piece . . .

It's about childhood.

My parents back in France spend their evenings watching television in the socks I sent them from London. I love my parents and forgive them. Above the couch is a framed watercolor of a mountain lion. If it fell, it would kill them. It's a limited-edition print. There are 199 others in the world.

They will only ever be my parents once. They are the only parents I will ever have in the history of the universe. I wonder if they feel me thinking about them here in Quebec City in the rain—I wonder if they feel me like a small animal gnawing them affectionately.

I continue up the hill. The Chateau Frontenac towers over the city like a benevolent dictator. From the eighteenth floor, you can see the Laurentian Mountains. Montreal is five hours southwest. The castle was built for well-to-do railroad passengers a few decades after the American Civil War. I suppose for some Quebecois, it's the biggest building they'll ever see. Lovers come here too and walk the city at dusk. You can see them on the promenade, sharing an umbrella, huddled together, stopping only to kiss and stare down at a cold black river dabbed with patches of streetlight.

When I play, I feel as though I am flying. I circle the auditorium. I am anywhere but inside my body. Without music, I would be a prisoner trapped in a sealed wall.

When I play, I sometimes picture my parents. And then the moment I finish playing, there is an eruption of applause. People cannot wait to give applause because they clap for themselves; they clap because they have been recognized by someone who died long ago in a room that flickered with candlelight.

I want to call my father, but my parents will both be in bed. They'll be annoyed if I call—but grateful tomorrow. My father thinks me eccentric anyway. He tells his friends at the café about me, about how eccentric I am. It's his way of talking about me.

In Noyant, the small French village where I grew up, it is too late to call anyone. I can feel the stillness of the town. The empty streets. My parents are asleep. The glowing numbers of the red alarm clock magnified by a glass set down in front of it. In the glass there are tiny bubbles that rise to the surface in the night. The remnants of supper will be in the refrigerator. There will be a cool skin of moisture on the car outside—a new Renault. My brother bought it for them as a Christmas present. I remember that my mother wanted to go for a drive in her nightgown; my brother was overjoyed with this. My father washed his hands and looked at it through the kitchen window before going outside. He stood next to it and put his hand on the roof. Then he went off to the vegetable patch beyond the far wall of the house and dug for a few forgotten potatoes. My mother took my brother inside and reassured him that we'd all go for a ride after breakfast. My brother has never understood our father. My brother is emotionally literal. Women have always loved him. I miss him. We grew up in a cottage that was part of a small bourgeois estate my father cared for.

The long eighteenth-century manor waits in darkness for its part-time occupants, who are spread across Paris for most of the year like different parts of a machine. They are a lovely family. Though one side is a little solemn, while the other is a little zealous. The house is long and white with many windows. In the attic there is a box of Napoleonic uniforms. In one of the bedrooms, three dozen Agatha Christie Penguin paperbacks. In another, engravings of birds.

Tomorrow I will return to New York, my home for almost a decade now. More concerts at the end of the week. One at the Lotos Club, another at a fund-raiser for Central Park, then Los Angeles—a concert at the Hollywood Bowl—then San Francisco, then Phoenix.

I love New York but miss the silence of rural Europe. Americans are literal. I think my brother would find a wife here in five minutes.

Bach's Suites for Solo Cello were written as pieces intended to teach but contain a mystery musicians unravel without knowing why; a map that shows the position of other maps. They are as popular as the stock pieces I play by Mozart and Haydn. Bach's Suites for Solo Cello are actually my biggest sellers. Bach and my brother helped buy my small apartment in Brooklyn. My brother doesn't know I know, but he bought thousands of copies of my CD and put them in his employees' Christmas bags. My brother's employees love him passionately. If there were a war on, they'd become his private army. It's amazing how he's done so well in business. He's crushed all competition. He's been on the cover of business magazines worldwide. For reasons known only to my brother and me, he has almost single-handedly made Renault the most popular brand of small car in Europe. I even have one here in New York. Everybody wants to know what it is. They always pronounce the "T". I have a mechanic in Queens. He's from Senegal and also grew up with Renault automobiles. In fact, I park it at his house and he uses it to drive his six kids around. I haven't seen it in almost two years. My brother doesn't know but would approve of the whole situation. My brother and I have the same brown Renault 16s, both from 1978. Perhaps we hold on to our childhoods because we can't hold on to each other. His girlfriends are always surprised when their millionaire boyfriend picks them up in a 1978 Renault 16.

An hour after my performance in Quebec City I walked right past my hotel into the maze of old streets. The rain was too beautiful to miss. Then I found Le Saint Amour, a little French restaurant. The food reminded me of home. I explained how I don't drink because I'm allergic, but the waiter brought little glasses of wine for me to sniff as I sank my fork into foie gras, filet mignon, truffled lentils. I'm not really allergic to alcohol; the opposite actually—my body loves the stuff.

The restaurant was packed with couples. A teenage girl sat quietly with her father. She was angry or disappointed with him. He knew it but pretended not to be bothered. I think all children are disappointed with their parents if they're lucky enough to get so close.

I left an enormous tip. I shall never forget my waiter. He kept trying to speak Italian, even though he knew I was French. He kept mentioning his daughters. He wore glasses that made him look too old. He loved being a waiter. He said that each meal was a memory. He said that he was a part of something good that had not started with him and would not end with him. As I left the restaurant, I felt a stabbing sadness. I would never see him again.

I passed several cold shops. Everything was closed. Puppets in a shop window stared out into the street, pretending not to see me. I walked carefully across the icy cobbles. It was snowing now, but only lightly. The buildings were silent, their occupants asleep inside. It was after one and so quiet I could hear the buzzing of streetlights as I walked under them.

The city looked different. I stood in the middle of the square before Notre-Dame-des-Victoires, a small gray, crooked church. They once filmed a sad film there. It was about a boy whose father was a failure. Going back somewhere at night is almost like haunting the world after death.

I kept walking, making eyes at the statues, naming each one like a sentimental drunkard after lovers and friends.

And then I stopped walking. My eye was drawn by movement. I couldn't quite see what it was—most likely a human figure passing before a dark window like a fish barely visible beneath the surface of a pond.

Each window held its very own candle. But they weren't real candles, just electric lights shaped like candles. The long house was tucked into an alley that glowed with snow. The streetlights at the far end of the house cast a great shadow on the side of the crooked church. The house was almost a smaller version of the one in which I had grown up—the bourgeois manor my father had spent his life maintaining like a mute first-born child. There were other windows too, ones without candles, ones so dark it was almost as if there were no glass at all. An inscription above the door read, "Par le Coeur de Mon Fils," and then a stone relief of a hand entering what appeared to be a human heart. Also, a large crucifix carved into the heavy wooden door. The order and cleanliness of the corridor that was visible through the only brightly lit window, on the ground floor, made me think this was a convent.

Then I saw the figure pass by the window again. It stopped. Whoever it was had seen me standing outside in the freezing air. It was past three in the morning. We were the only two inhabitants of an entire city; footprints on each other's island.

The figure swiftly moved to another window, one with a candle, and I saw who it was.

I could distinguish her profile, but details remained a mystery. She stood with the poise of someone young. Her hand pressed up against the pane. Then, in the mist which had laid itself thinly upon the early morning glass—as if solely for the purpose of what was about to happen next— this woman whom I knew but would never know, this lost, sleepless figure who found herself wandering the corridors of an icy dawn, wrote something very slowly with her finger upon the pane. Then she lifted the candle against the letters she had drawn with her finger:

Allez

I took my hands out of my pockets. It began to rain and she disappeared. I turned and walked slowly away.

I said the word over and over again as I paced the city. And I felt suddenly warm, full of strength, full of life, and ready to give life. I suppose I need people to tell me what I already know.

My father and mother would be awake by now.

The kitchen sink full of vegetables freshly pulled from the earth.

My brother in Paris reading beside the window—his new girlfriend still asleep.

And Sandy, my agent—with her daughter in their hot bed, nestled in one another's arms. Their breathing is soft and private; mouths open against hillsides of pillow.

I must have returned to my hotel room around breakfast time the next day. I was out all night in the cold and soaked through. I left a small pool in the elevator. The couple staying on my floor with the miniature poodle will probably be blamed. The staff here is very gracious, and the grand Chateau Frontenac hotel is like something from the mind of Chekhov.

I am now soaking in a hot bath.

My chest protrudes from the bubbles like an island upon which the carved head of some great deity has come to life. I must remember to write in my diary that I spent the early hours of the morning making eyes at all the statues in the city and then soaked in a tub.

My shoes were so wet they had ceased to make a sound on the cobbles. I have put them in the sink. The leather is impossibly tender now; I don't think it will ever go back to normal. I think of the word. I can feel her finger moving across my back in the shape of letters.

Allez

When I get back to New York, I'm going to start getting up early. I'm going to invite my brother to come and see me. We will sit together in the park in heavy coats. We will watch the clouds pass. Sometimes I imagine that each cloud holds the weight of what will happen.

The water in my bath is cooling. I can see a version of myself in it. My eyes ascend to the window, then through it. They find the river and follow it. Quebec City was taken from its ancient people by the French when William Shakespeare was about my age. My hotel room overlooks the St. Lawrence River. Chunks of ice slip by with the current. Quebec women once set out hard rods of corn on planks of wood on the river's bank. I can see their cotton-white breath and their gray teeth as glimmering fish are spread across barrels. Their aprons are wet. Frost has dusted white the rich brown earth. The ground is hard as stone. Cold has cracked their hands. They laugh and wave to children on small boats drifting. Clouds churn in the eyes of the fish.

I like my room here at the Chateau. It overlooks part of

the river but is directly over a park. In the park there are trees stripped by winter and blackened by rain. I can't stop thinking of the early settlers of the 1600s. The smell of wet leather. Stupid horses not doing what they're told. Babies crying. Wet wood. Ice on everything, ice cutting through the body. The earth too frozen to bury the dead. And nothing will grow. A few frozen berries dot the woods like eyes. New foods are tried but result in sickness.

I must have fallen asleep in the tub. I awake to a light tapping on my door. I don't answer and hope the person will go away. Tapping again. Perhaps my cello is ready to come up from the hotel vault they assured me exists. I find a towel, open the door, and thank the bellboy with some money. He asks if I want breakfast, then says it was an honor to carry my instrument. He walks away whistling. I think the staff like me. Two chambermaids think they heard me practicing in my room before my concert yesterday, but it wasn't me. It was Pablo Casals. I was playing one of his old recordings, a Toccata in C Major by J. S. Bach. They were shuffling outside the door. I made it louder. When it finished, they clapped. I should write to Bose and tell them their speakers are a success.

Most people never get to hear this music. Music helps us understand where we have come from but, more importantly, what has happened to us. Bach wrote the Cello Suites for his young wife as an exercise to help her learn the cello. But inside each note is the love we are unable to express with words. I can feel her frustration and joy as my bow carves out the notes of the mild-mannered organist who saw composing as one of his daily chores. When Bach died, some of his children sold his scores to the butcher; they had decided the paper was more useful for wrapping meat. In a small village in Germany, a father brought home a limp goose wrapped in paper that was covered with strange and beautiful symbols.

I open my cello case and smell my grandfather. I pick up the instrument and run my fingers tenderly up and down the strings. In each note of music lives every tragedy of the world and every moment of its salvation. The cellist Pablo Casals knew this. Music is only a mystery to people who want it explained. Music and love are the same.

I am staring at the fireplace in my room, holding my cello. I think of my parents again. My father doesn't listen to the music I record, but he sometimes comes to my performances when I'm in Tours or Saumur.

In my cello case is a mitten that belonged to the baker's daughter. I keep it in my pocket when I play. We sat next to each other in class. Her name was Anna. She had freckles and held her pencil with three fingers and a thumb.

Winter strips the village of my youth, but in spring the parks fill up again with children learning how to ride bicycles and not doing what they're told.

II

T O SEE HIM IS a miracle. He stands at the fountain and
gently raises a hand. Then birds swoop down from
trees and perch on his shoulders. Some hover, then drop into
his hands like soft stones. Children cry with joy. Parents
want to know who he is. They call him the birdman of Beverly Hills and talk about him over dinners with friends who
wonder what his story is. Some say his wife and child were
killed. Others say he was in a war. Many people believe he's
an eccentric billionaire.

He wears a dusty dinner jacket, and his pants are short
enough to clearly see white socks. His hair is overgrown, with
streaks of silver. Worn chestnut loafers tell of a different life.

Sometimes the birdman will raise a hand to his mouth
and whisper something to the plump bird cupped there. Moments later, the bird will fly out and land on someone in the
crowd: a boy's shoulder or the outstretched hand of a girl.

One Friday morning, not one but three birds landed on
an old man's knee. He was sad because no one had asked him
out to lunch that day, nor had he received any letters. When
the birds landed on him, his mouth trembled and the clouds
in his eyes parted.

When the birds flew away, he said, "What a nice birthday present!" The birdman nodded. The old man immediately went home, put away the length of rope, and went
downstairs to ask his young Mexican neighbor to be his

guest for dinner. They talked about many things. And over dessert the old man made a promise that he would teach his neighbor to read. They were both drunk. Every idea felt original. The next day, the neighbor took the old man a present and a piñada purchased in an East L.A. bakery next to the old Cat & Dog Hospital.

By the time the Mexican boy could read, the two of them had found that they fit the way jigsaw pieces do. They celebrated holidays together. They created for each other a world within a world and cast each other as stars.

Hope is the greatest of all gifts.

Once, a black-haired woman and her child asked the birdman his name. He sighed slowly. He didn't like questions. But the birds around him fluttered their wings. The tired woman and her young child peered up at the birdman.

"Please," the child implored. "Won't you tell us your name?"

The woman and child were holding hands. The afternoon sunshine warmed the tops of their heads. The woman tilted her left foot to the side as though pouring something out.

"Jonathan," the birdman said. Then he turned and walked away.

The birds flew with Jonathan, as though pulling his slight frame to the edge of the park with thin ropes. The park returned to normal. A homeless woman fell asleep to the sound of passing cars. Squirrels chased each other around tree trunks with acorns in their mouths.

III

S IX MONTHS LATER, THE black-haired woman told her
sister about the birdman over lunch at the Beverly Hills
Hotel.

"The birdman finally spoke and told us his name was
Jonathan," she said, laughing.

A woman sipping tea at the next table dropped her cup.
It split neatly in two parts on the saucer. Tea escaped into
the linens. A knot of waiters rushed out from behind a door.
The stains would be hard to remove.

The woman at the next table stood up and quickly stepped
toward the restrooms. She was wearing an old-fashioned
sequin skirt and forest-green shoes. She had grown up in
Wales. Her brother's name was also Jonathan.

It was almost five o'clock. Outside, the afternoon—heavy
with heat—listed like an old ship and people rolled from
one side of the city to the other.

The Beverly Hills Hotel is opulent. It prides itself on
many things. There is a salon and several places to eat. For
anyone who likes pink, it's paradise. In the bathroom, the
woman who lost her teacup sat in the stall and sobbed. She
could picture the waiters cleaning up; there would soon be
fresh linens and shining silverware. Within a few minutes,
all traces of her outburst would be erased.

The woman felt acorns in her pocket. She squeezed each
one of them. Her Jonathan collected nuts. He kept them in

small bowls around his bedroom. He wanted to feed the birds. He was obsessed with birds. And they built nests outside his bedroom in small dark places in the roof. He said he could see their eyes peering into his bedroom at night. Perhaps they knew all along what would happen to him. That was long ago in Wales, in a one-eyed village of sheep, mud, and stars.

Grief is a country where it rains and rains but nothing grows. The dead live somewhere else——wearing the clothes we remember them in.

IV

WHEN BABY JONATHAN CAME home from the hospital wrapped in white, I couldn't stop looking at him. I would sit by him at night. His breaths were fast and small. When his arms were strong enough, he reached for me, his sister.

Our house was a cottage warmed by hot coals that burned slowly and deeply in the kitchen stove. In summer the fireplaces in the main rooms were dark and full of winter's ashes. My mother would make salad sandwiches with lettuce from the garden. When Jonathan could walk, I took him into the fields behind our cottage and sat him down on a towel somewhere shady. I would build tiny huts from mud and straw as he held in his chubby fingers the brown plastic mice we both knew were our friends.

On Saturdays we would all go into the village. Outside the butcher's shop whole animals hung from hooks of brushed steel. Jonathan would point but had yet to find words.

When it was hot, I would take off his clothes and bounce him on the bed. I like to think this was his first memory.

My dolls sat in the toy box until Jonathan was two and he found them. Then began the great age of dressing them up. The two dolls became our younger siblings. Once we wrapped them in aluminum foil and pretended they were robots. Our quiet father would send the dolls postcards from wherever he traveled on business. I would read them to the dolls, and Jonathan would nod and then put them to bed, saying, "Wasn't that nice? A postcard from somewhere you'll never go."

When he began wearing underpants, he got in the habit of tying his unused diapers on the dolls. His underpants were small. When I came home from school, if I found them on the living room floor, soiled, I knew he would be crying on the bed waiting for me. I would take off my underwear and run it under the faucet and then show it to him. He would stop crying. All siblings have a secret life from their parents. Parents love their children, but children need each other to negotiate the strange forest they find themselves in.

It wasn't long before I was caught in the act. Jonathan stood naked at the bathroom door as I doused my underwear with cold water. He approached and wrapped his little body around my legs. The bathroom window held the final square of daylight. It was very bright and also very still. Downstairs, we could hear the sounds of cartoons pouring from the television. Jonathan never cried again when he had an accident. I firmly believe that while lies and deception destroy love, they can also build and defend it. Love requires imagination more than experience.

Nobody knows when Jonathan died. My father saw something in the snow from the bathroom window one morning. I wasn't allowed to go outside, so I sat in the bathroom and ripped out my hair. When my mother saw clumps of it on my bare legs, she decided to let me see Jonathan's body. I screamed and screamed and never stopped screaming until I met a man named Bruno Bonnet.

V

ARRIVING IN THE DARK for my concert the next day, I find Los Angeles pulsating with traffic; pairs of red lights thread the valleys with their flat houses and clear pools. The oldest houses have round edges and crumble a little more whenever the ground shakes. In the suburbs, imagine all-night Laundromats heavy with the freshness of clean clothes; young mothers with plastic flowers in their hair. Babies peer up through black eyes from hot towels. Gangs of men turn their heads to eat tacos at a roadside cantina. Trash blows from one side of the highway to the other, then back again.

Farther north, approaching Hollywood—hot-dog stands with neon arrows and faded paint; tattooed women with chopped black hair buying lip gloss at Hollywood pharmacies; a homeless man pushes a shopping cart full of shoes but he is barefoot. He keeps looking behind. His stomach hangs out. Sometime in the 1960s he was delivered into the trembling hands of his mother. If only it could happen again. Los Angeles is a place where dreams balance forever on the edge of coming true. A city on a cliff held fast by its own weight.

I like performing here, especially at the Hollywood Bowl. There's something about the movement of air. My music fills the thermals, and I imagine the notes flooding the city like birds. It's hot here too; a real contrast to Quebec City two weeks ago, where my feet froze after walking the city at night and conversing with the statuary. When my shoes dried, they were very stiff. I put them in a clear plastic bag and labeled it "Le Flâneur de Quebec." I think it's important to keep items of clothing that have emotional significance.

I've been thinking about that woman I saw behind the window in the middle of the night. Since that evening I've felt differently about a lot of things. I spoke to my brother about it. He thinks I'm finally coming around. He thinks I suffer from depression. But I'm just quiet. Solitude and depression are like swimming and drowning. In school many years ago, I learned that flowers sometimes unfold inside themselves.

After a good night's sleep, it's lunchtime and I'm eating meat loaf in the Beverly Hills Hotel. It's actually late morning. Outside on the patio is a Brazilian spearmint tree that died years ago. The waiter said it's now over a hundred years old—but does a thing continue to accrue years once it's dead? If so, if so . . . I stop myself. There are stumps of baguette on the table. The baker enters my mind. He is drying his hands on an apron. I stop myself.

Later, I will sink again.

Later, I will row myself out to sea with my bow to Anna's floating body. I can see her face so clearly. She died when she was twelve. I was thirteen. She hasn't aged with me, but sometimes I imagine her as a woman.

"A girl comes every week." The waiter was back, still thinking about the tree outside. "She plays with the plastic ferns in the branches."

I look into the branches and smile.

"Landscapers look at it and laugh," he said. "To them it must look stupid."

I like waiters—but you have to win them over quickly before you become just another client, just another table 23. The meat loaf is mediocre here, but the service is fabulous. I seldom eat at home; I'm on the road so much. This hotel is like having an adoring mother who can't cook.

The most delicious bread in the world is made in my village. It's something to do with salt in the water. The baker's daughter and I used to ride our bicycles to the edge of town. Remember that Noyant is a small village. We would leave our bikes leaning against each other as we climbed the swaying gate into the soft fields of Farmer Ricard.

He was a large man with eyes that seemed ready to fall out. His lips were very large too, and he wore green army sweaters. He once carried a baby cow on his back through waist-deep snow across several kilometers of fields. The vet in the next village was drinking chamomile tea and looking out the window. A broken leg was set and healed in a barn warmed by gaslight. Everyone in the village remembers what happened. The cow was allowed to die of old age.

Farmer Ricard has a photograph of his father in the

kitchen. He was in the Resistance and was tortured to death. Madame Ricard is in the habit of talking to the photograph while Farmer Ricard is away in the fields. Sometimes she can hear him hammering in the barn. He likes to drink his coffee with both hands. They haven't made love for years but sleep holding hands.

A pianist here at the hotel is playing "The Girl from Ipanema." Lights behind the bar make the liquor glow. My napkin is pebbled at the edges. The hotel crest is faintly impressed in the center. The dining room is mostly empty. The dining room is split into many areas. Three tables over, an old man is doing magic tricks for his teenage grand-daughter. It looks like she is wearing her prom dress. Her hair is pulled back. Her earrings are new. Every time the knife disappears into the napkin, she smiles.

At another table are a young Mexican and a very old man with white hair. They are reading from the same book and eating from the same bowl of ice cream.

This is the sort of place where pictures were snapped before the war. Glossy black-and-white prints now hanging in Beverly Hills above quiet beds in bedrooms that smell of mothballs. Women in black gloves. Smoking men with shiny hair. Palm trees in the background. Glasses, empty of gin, replenished by melting ice.

Once we were in Farmer Ricard's misty field, the baker's daughter and I would fill our pockets with stones. If one of us remembered to bring a plastic bag, that was even better. When laden with more stones than we could possibly carry, we dragged our heavy bodies to the edge of the field and made a pile. Then we'd split up and the search would continue.

We collected stones to save the plows.

Monsieur Ricard gave us a franc for every ten stones. If we managed to find one too big for one of us to carry alone (that was the test), that particular stone was worth a franc all by itself. When we got tired, we'd sit on the dirt and watch birds. Sometimes a farm cat would find us and its tail would go up. The cat would often turn around to look at something that wasn't there. For the past twenty-two years, I've been doing the same thing.

When I finish my lunch, I'm going downstairs to the Beverly Hills Hotel gift shop. It's opposite the hair salon. Rows of women sit with twists of silver foil in their hair. The stylists talk about celebrities, and soon the women start to feel like celebrities.

In the hotel gift shop I'm going to buy a hatbox.

Then I'm going to fill it with stones.

VI

FOR JONATHAN'S FOURTH BIRTHDAY, he was given a white hardcover book called *The British Book of Birds*. This was by far his favorite possession. When he was upset, he would clumsily sketch birds from the book, gripping his colored pencil in a fist.

About this time we had some lovely family vacations together.

Watching my father lift the caravan onto the hitch of our family sedan was like watching Atlas take up the world on his back. Then, on the motorway, my brother and I nesting in the back as my mother's hand appeared behind the seat with a smile of orange for each of us, my father quietly navigating our fortress to a field on a hillside at a distance from our Welsh village unfathomable to us.

By the evening, my mother, father, Jonathan, and I would be sitting in plastic chairs under a Cinzano umbrella somewhere on the Welsh coast. The smell of my father's cold lager beer, my mother's wine, cigarette smoke from another table. The sound of cars in the town, the smell of fish and chips, women in heels clopping along the narrow roads to the town nightclub. Then back at the caravan, Jonathan and I in bunk beds. We communicated by gently knocking on the thin wall against which our beds were built. The blankets were always musty, and the smell of dinner sometimes lingered until morning.

As an adult, I've realized where Jonathan found his gentleness. Our father was a shy, good-natured boy—a handsome man from South Wales, strong enough to lift a caravan by the throat but wise enough to cup a moth as it slid its body against the flickering black-and-white TV. I remember the release from our caravan through a cracked door into the dark field, as though on its powdery back balanced the weight of his children's dreams.

The day was spent exploring the village and the countryside. My favorite memory is cooking sausages beside a river. We hiked through shallow woods and didn't see anyone. My mother grew up afraid because of what people did to her. And then afraid of what they might do to us. To her family she was shy, loving, secretive, and fiercely loyal, but in the world she stood poised, cunning, and glamorous. The perfect saleswoman.

I remember holding her slender hand as we crossed a river somewhere close to the sea, our caravan back through the forest on a concrete slab with other caravans. Little Jonathan held my hand. One of his shoes was wet. He had misjudged his steps. We all thought it was funny.

I wish I'd kept his shoes—that's one thing I regret getting rid of. I loved those shoes, and I loved the socks too.

And then my father with sausages wrapped in newspaper, who had not yet reached the bank. I remember our faces changing before us as we crossed the cold, blind, rushing river. I led Jonathan, carefully picking out stones whose heads poked out from the water, as though they wished to say something.

I remember looking back for my father, slowed by the weight of his joy from knowing that we were somewhere but he could not see us. I remember my mother's trembling voice as we neared the other bank and Jonathan's laughter like a tablecloth spread over his fear. Then my father tilted across on the stones, and we cooked sausages beside the water.

Jonathan disappeared that winter. It was a few days before Christmas. I remember asking my mother where he was. She told me to look under his bed. Potatoes boiled. The kitchen was full of steam. I wiped the window with my sleeve.

"He won't be outside, dear—look at the snow."

I will never forget that moment. Because he was outside.

My father had left a ladder propped against a conifer tree.

He was cutting branches with a chain saw before the snow came.

Jonathan had climbed the ladder. Nobody knew.

Once in the tree, he climbed and climbed. We don't know why. Perhaps he knew he had come to the end of his life and wanted to become a bird.

I hope he did become a bird.

I hear him call every morning from the tree outside my apartment.

By late afternoon we were all worried. My mother telephoned the police. My father searched the village, then young men showed up at our doorstep with flashlights and heavy walking sticks.

I fell asleep in the early hours of the morning without wanting to. I've felt guilty about that for most of my life. Perhaps if I'd stayed awake, I would have heard him call out.

The next morning several old Land Rovers with canvas backs were parked outside. The men at the kitchen table drank strong tea. Eggs spat in the frying pan. The farmers' waxed jackets dripped water on the stone floor.

They had found nothing and were half-frozen.

Dogs on the floor at their feet.

The dogs refused the bacon scraps offered them. The men said the dogs were sad because they couldn't find the boy. The scent of him lingered in their noses.

On Christmas Day, we sat and looked at the presents. My mother cried and threw her shoe through a window. I prayed by reading Jonathan's *British Book of Birds* aloud to the heavens. It responded in a scatter of soft white tongues that told us nothing.

In January, two weeks later, my father was shaving when he noticed a speck in the garden outside.

A smudge of color broke the white monotony.

Without wiping the shaving cream that smeared his cheeks, he rushed outside into the thick snow. Jonathan's body lay completely still. The branch onto which he had climbed and become trapped had broken that night in a storm. He lay in the snow faceup. His body was hard and his mouth was open. In one of his hands were three frozen acorns. In his mind, it was not yet Christmas Day.

It's still a mystery why he didn't call out. Perhaps he was afraid of being punished; children possess the most powerful fear of disappointing their parents.

After they took Jonathan's body away, my father went into the shed. He closed the door and then chopped off his right hand with an axe.

The police came and took him to hospital.

For almost three decades, I've kept acorns in my pockets. I check for them constantly.

Sometimes I roll them in my palms and hear laughter, then the sound of a breaking branch, something soft punching the snow from a great height.

Birdsong.

VII

THE GIRLS IN THE gift shop at the Beverly Hills Hotel were kind enough to help me pack the stones into the hatbox with pink tissue paper. They asked if I was French. They said it wasn't so much my accent as the way I was dressed. They were excited to be involved in something eccentric.

The younger of the two wore blue eye shadow. She asked me what *"Voulez-vous coucher avec moi"* means. The older woman giggled and said she just wants me to say it. The girl with blue eye shadow slapped her friend's arm.

I asked for more tissue paper, and the younger girl asked why I wanted to wrap stones anyway. I told her it was just something I did.

Before I closed the hatbox, the young shop assistant reached in. I waited with the lid in my hands.

"Stones are really quite beautiful, aren't they?" she said. Her retainer glinted in the shop light.

I walked past the hair salon and then up the stairs. As I passed the Polo Lounge, a woman appeared from around a corner and walked straight into me. The force of her motion was enough to knock me down. I dropped the hatbox, and the stones rolled out with a loud clacking sound. The woman was carrying what I thought were small rocks, and they fell from her hands and scattered across the hard, glossy floor.

She glared at me. And then suddenly an arm of sunlight reached through a high window and opened its hand upon her face. I saw her eyes as clearly as if we had been pressed against one another in a very small space.

A bellboy rushed over and started to pick up her stones.

"Acorns!" he exclaimed.

The woman looked at him in horror.

"Please, I'll do it," she said. The bellboy was confused and continued to pick up the acorns, just more carefully.

"No, I'll do it, please," the woman said again. The bell-boy looked at me for a few moments and then hurried off.

For some reason I didn't get up immediately. Instead, I watched her collect her acorns. She had beautiful shoes. And then the sunlight fell away and I noticed drops were falling from her eyes. I finally stood up and proceeded to collect the five stones I'd so carefully packed into the hatbox with the girls downstairs in the shop.

"Sorry," the woman said genuinely.

She had an accent I had never heard. Her hair was very soft, but I kept looking at her shoes.

For a few moments we stood opposite one another. It was awkward. Neither of us walked away. To anyone watching, it must have looked as though we were talking—but we weren't saying anything.

The most significant conversations of our lives occur in silence.

"I'm so sorry," she said again. I said I was sorry too. I wasn't sorry, but I felt like I should have been.

There were freckles on her cheeks and forehead. Her eyes were very green.

When she walked off, I sat on a bench by the counter and held on to my box. I sat there for some time and even considered leaving my box behind so that I might follow her, grab her arm, and force her to go somewhere with me and sit down. I wanted only to look at her green eyes and to hear the lilting song of her voice, as though her words were the notes I had been searching for, the vital sounds that I had never played.

The most important notes in music are the ones that wait until sound has entered the ear before revealing their true nature. They are the spaces between the sounds that blow through the heart, knocking things over.

I eventually went back to my room.

Later. My telephone flashing. A message from Sandy, my agent, some detail about my San Francisco concert and the music director's belief that my grandfather's chair is too damaged to sit on. I wanted to call her and tell her about this woman but felt for some reason it would upset her. Her daughter's birthday is coming up. Sandy asked if I would buy her a bicycle. Her daughter requested that I give her a bicycle and teach her how to ride it. I think when I am older I will be someone she turns to when her mother is depressed. I think Sandy is depressed a lot. More than once I've found her sitting at her desk in the dark.

I remember when my parents bought me a bike. In Europe of the 1970s, there was less production of things and so many of my toys and clothes were secondhand. In my village there was a weekend before Christmas when people sold bicycles. They leaned them against the wall of the church. From each handlebar hung a tag with the price in francs and the name of the person selling it. So if a child had outgrown a bicycle, on Christmas Eve it would begin a new life. Twenty or so bicycles circulated the village, changing owners every few years.

Sometimes, previous owners, unable to contain themselves, would call out to their old bicycles as they passed at the mercy of new owners.

"Isn't she a beauty—but watch for the front brake!" or "Be careful going over curbs like that—you'll buckle the wheels!"

It's amazing the details from childhood that can surface in a day. That's the best present I ever received. I remember watching parents walk the line of bicycles leaned up against the church, feeling for the money in their pockets, and the children who sat excitedly at home—forbidden to follow, even at a distance.

My bicycle was golden brown with a dynamo light—a small wheel spun by the back wheel that's connected to a small cylinder that uses the motion to power the front and rear lights.

I called Sandy and told her about my first bicycle.

"You get worse every day," she said. "But you're still my favorite client."

We straightened out the details for the afternoon concert in San Francisco. No chair, no concert, I told her. Then I tried to call my brother. His assistant picked up his cell phone and told me that he had gone shooting.

"Shooting?" I said.

"But he isn't shooting," the assistant said, "he's just in the forest with English."

I laughed. "English" was what my brother called his current girlfriend's father because he wore corduroy pants with small pheasants embroidered into the material.

"So English," my brother mocked.

"He's always glad when you call," his assistant said, and then she hung up without saying good-bye.

I never know when to hang up the phone, and try to say one final good-bye even though I can hear the other person has gone.

Then I ran a bath and let the heat settle. Before I slipped

into the still water, I thought of the woman who walked into me downstairs. And suddenly I felt an extraordinary sense of hope for everything that was to come, a continuation of what I had begun feeling in Quebec City. It was something I had not experienced since I was a boy. Something I hadn't felt since the days of sitting in fields.

VIII

WHO IS THIS MAN, who like an apparition haunts my every thought? I thought about him last night in my small, steamy apartment. I took out my photographs of Jonathan and spread them on the kitchen table. Then I went to sleep and dreamed that the man from the hotel was sitting on the edge of my bed. Then I was watching the scene from above, and in the place of my body was stone. A person made of rock in the shape of me.

I thought about him this morning sipping coffee on the patio next to the pool no one ever swims in. There are leaves at the bottom. This man's face is like the end of a book, or the beginning of one.

If I thought I would see him in the park, I perhaps would not have gone. But the urge to see this birdman—another Jonathan . . . or my Jonathan. You never know.

You understand I had to make sure. Grief is sometimes a quiet but obsessive madness. Coincidences are something too great to ignore.

When I arrived at the park, I was of course too early. A few people slumbered under blankets beside their shopping carts. I stopped and looked at a homeless woman. The ridges on her cheeks were so deep her face could have been a map; the story of what happened. I wanted to touch it but didn't. She was somewhere far away in sleep, swimming back to the park through a dream.

All parks are beautiful when quiet and you see things like a book forgotten on a bench read by the wind. Other things too: Someone must have shed their shoes to walk in the grass and then forgotten about them. The shoes had remained neatly arranged for the duration of a night, jewels at their center. I wondered why nobody had taken them.

I chose a bench close to the fountain.

An hour later the birdman arrived. He was much too old to be my brother. And his skin was dark and cracked. His nose was wide and bulged awkwardly from a thin face. The whites of his eyes were impossibly white, but their centers were black. His clothes were beautiful but ruined. How strange that I was actually disappointed it was not my Jonathan. Another way to punish myself, to look behind for someone I feel but cannot see.

And then I noticed the man across the park. At first I wasn't sure if it was him, but then he looked at me and I was sure. He was more handsome than I remembered, and there was something serious in his movements—in the way he sat. A person with important messages but who has lost all memory of where he is going. And then I gasped because that was a description of me. Perhaps all my opinions of other people are opinions of another self.

I don't know why, but I wasn't surprised to see him. His legs were crossed neatly as though it were his favorite way of sitting. He didn't seem surprised to see me either.

Then children arrived and stood around the birdman. They shuffled their sandals in the dust.

He'd dropped his box of stones when I bumped into him. I can't understand how he fell over; I didn't think our impact was so hard. Perhaps he was off-balance. Perhaps he had been waiting all along for someone to knock him down and allow him to drop the weight he'd so faithfully carried.

For an hour or so, we both watched the birdman, laughing intermittently. I noticed he had a baguette next to him and wondered if he'd brought it to feed the birds. The birds flew around the children's heads, seemingly at the control of the birdman. They flew in arcs as though held with strings. The children laughed and jumped. They also looked at one another.

I glanced over at the man often and he looked at me too. It was inevitable that we meet. Like rivers, we had been flowing on a course for one another.

And so, at some point I stood up and walked over to his bench. My shoes crunching the small stones. I counted the steps. My heart bursting from my chest. I sat down and looked at his hands. He looked surprised and I wasn't sure what to do. My hand began to shake and he reached for it. I let him. With his other hand, he took from his pocket a handful of acorns and put them in my palm.

From my pocket I took a large stone and set it squarely in his open hand. If there is such a thing as marriage, it takes place long before the ceremony: in a car on the way to the airport; or as a gray bedroom fills with dawn, one lover watching the other; or as two strangers stand together in the rain with no bus in sight, arms weighed down with shopping bags. You don't know then. But later you realize—— *that* was the moment.

And always without words.

Language is like looking at a map of somewhere. Love is living there and surviving on the land.

How could two people know each other so intimately without ever having told the old stories? You get to an age where the stories don't matter anymore, and the stories once told so passionately become a tide that never quite reaches the point of being said. And there is no such thing as fate, but there are no accidents either.

I didn't fall in love with Bruno then. I had always loved him and we were always together.

Love is like life but starts before and continues after—— we arrive and depart in the middle.

IX

M Y FATHER ONCE TOLD me that coincidences mean you're on the right path. When the woman who bumped into me at the Beverly Hills Hotel approached my bench and sat down, I didn't know what was going to happen, and I didn't care. I only had the feeling that I always wanted to be with her. I had no urge to tell her anything— there was no need; she knew everything she needed to know without having to learn it.

As we sat side by side in the park, two birds dropped upon our knees. The birdman was looking at us. The children were looking at us too. The woman didn't move. She just stared at her bird, but her bird was staring at me. The small bird on my knee didn't seem to be thinking anything. Then he turned and looked at me. He rubbed his beak together and it made a sawing sound. I think he was asking for a seed.

When one of the youngest children in the group screamed, the birdman whistled and the birds flew from us back to his outstretched arms.

"Did you know this would happen?" I asked.

"It's why I came," she said. I drank down her voice.

"Are you French?"

"The baguette gave it away?"

She smiled.

"Would you like some?" I offered it.

She shook her head. "It looks too precious."

I ripped its hat off and she took it. She ripped it in half and gave me some. A scatter of pigeons suddenly swooped down.

"Where are you from?"

"The mountains of North Wales." She bit her lip. "Have you heard of Wales?"

"*Oui.*"

"Good," she said. "I can take you if you have warm clothes and like sausages."

For an hour we sat watching the many people who walked past.

Then she said:

"What are we going to do?"

I liked that she asked this. It meant we felt the same way about one another. I was still holding the stone she had given me. She had put the acorns I gave her into a pocket.

"I'm performing in San Francisco tomorrow night— will you come?"

"Who are you?" she said. "Tell me your name at least— I don't make a habit of following strange men around."

We both looked at the birdman.

"Really?" I said.

When she laughed, her eyes closed slightly.

"Bruno," I said. "This is my name, and I am just a small boy from a French village who can play the cello."

She seemed content with this answer. But then said hastily:

"Maybe it's the cello that plays you."

Then she added:

"I think you must be a very good cellist—a gifted one even."

"Why?" I asked.

"Because you're like a key that unlocks people."

"I doubt that."

"Not just people," she added.

She seemed suddenly confused, the way a woman does when she feels in danger of saying too much.

"What's your name?" I asked.

She smiled. "You could ask me that every day and get a different answer."

She bit her nail and looked away.

"That's not a very good response, is it?"

"It's perfect," I said, and meant it.

"Well, my name is Hannah."

The present grows within the boundaries of the past.

I asked if she had plans for the weekend. I couldn't believe I was inviting her to San Francisco—that I was allowing someone to trespass into my life, to climb over the gate and start across the farmland to the small cottage where I had been living for decades with just my music, my stones, my baguettes; a mitten.

I thought of the woman I had seen in Quebec City behind the icy window, the nun who wrote the word in the glass.

No beauty without decay. I read that somewhere else.

Every moment is the paradox of now or never.

If my brother back in France could have witnessed this event in the park with Hannah, he would have cried for joy. He cries a lot, and women love that about him, but then he can be stubborn and macho, and they love that too. I can imagine telling him about Hannah. He'll want to fly out and meet her. He'll want to send her flowers, chocolates, cheese—give her the latest Renault convertible. I can see them strolling the fields of Noyant, arm in arm, my brother picking up sticks to throw.

"Come to San Francisco," I say. "Fly up for my concert in the afternoon and we'll rent a car and drive back to Los Angeles together—this is where you live?"

"Yes," she said. "I have a shop in Silver Lake that sells prints, posters, and paintings."

"Of birds?"

"I wish it were just birds—but not everyone is like me."

"I think I like who you are."

"Well, it's not what I chose," she said.

I felt mild humiliation—as if *I* were somehow a part of what she hadn't wanted.

Then I said:

"Sometimes I think it's life that chooses us—and here we are thinking that we're steering the ship, when we're just vehicles for an elaborate division of life."

"Then why can it end so easily?" she said.

I wasn't sure what she meant. I risked an answer anyway.

"It ends quickly so that we value it," I said.

She turned her whole body to face me.

"No, Bruno, we value it because it's like that—but why is it like that? Why can life suddenly fly away when those left behind have so much to say? So much that silence is like a mouthful of cotton—but then when it's time to speak, one is capable only of silence. So much that's left undone. What happens to all the things a person would have done?"

I had considered all this.

"I'm not sure I want to know anything anymore," I said.

She bit her lip. I could tell she wanted to know everything.

We continued talking. Many of the things I said to Hannah in those first, long, heavy days just formed in my mouth without much thought. They formed silently like clouds and then rained down upon her. When we talked, I realized I knew things I hadn't thought I knew.

She agreed to come to San Francisco. And we would drive back to Los Angeles along the cliff—the very edge of a country we had lived in for so long.

Before I walked her to the parking lot, Hannah said she wanted to give the birdman something she'd brought.

We approached him, and the children stepped back to give us room. From her pocketbook Hannah produced a tattered volume. A book. She handed it to the birdman.

It was *The British Book of Birds.*

"Look inside," Hannah told him.

He did.

It read:

> *To our dearest child, Jonathan,*
> *May the birds you love always love you back*

"See—this book belongs to you," Hannah said sweetly.

"No, young lady," the birdman said. "It belongs to you— but you don't belong to it."

He leaned in very close to her.

"You belong to you," he said.

X

WE WERE TWO PEOPLE in a car not speaking. I think it was a French writer who said that we perceive when love begins and when it declines by our embarrassment while alone together.

Hannah flew up to San Francisco for the concert. It took place in the afternoon. There were more children present than usual because of the time. As I drew each note from the instrument, I could sense her out there, watching, listening—biting her lip.

Anna's form appeared as always, but it felt far away. When I turned to look, I could see only the outline of her body. She was leaving me, and I wasn't surprised. I wondered where she would go. I would miss her in a new way.

We left San Francisco that afternoon by driving in a straight line over hills. The reflection off the water made the light seem golden; many of the houses were red and wore small towers at their corners. People sat in parks and drank water from plastic bottles. A man in a black T-shirt walked his dog and chatted on a cell phone. A girl on a bicycle ticked past. Her basket was full of lemons. Her hair was very curly. The sidewalk cafés were packed. Faces hidden by newspapers. Groups waiting for a table.

Our car moved forward slowly—it took hours to get out of San Francisco, but we were together, the only two passengers on a journey where the destination was unimportant. Hannah talked about my concert. She said she was the only person not clapping at the end. She said that for her the concert would never end.

When we turned true south onto the Pacific Coast Highway, Hannah said nothing for quite some time. I thought she was enjoying the scenery. A motorcycle passed us. Then we caught up to an RV and drove slowly behind it for several miles.

I began to ask Hannah questions, but she answered only with a word or two. I told her about the Metropolitan Museum of Art in New York—about the long fountain full of coins.

"I wonder how many of those wishes have come true," she said.

More silence.

"Do you hear that?" I asked.

"What?" she said. "I don't hear anything."

"That's the sound of keys on my ring," I said. "Sooner or later I'll find the one that unlocks you."

She didn't say anything but placed her hand on top of mine.

I took several very sharp curves, and then the road straightened out.

I looked at the sea. I thought of fish bobbing along the bottom. The motion of weeds.

Then Hannah said, "I want to tell you about Jonathan."

And little by little, his life was placed before me like a map with a small and beautiful country at its center.

I saw him with his book in the garden, sketching.

Then a body stretched out in the snow.

The fist of acorns.

The severed hand of her father in the shed.

The dumb hanging ladder.

Years later:

The many meals that would sit in front of her mother and turn cold.

The guilt of her father as he'd laugh at something on the television, then suddenly stop laughing and leave the room.

One night, Hannah said, he went out in his socks, took the chain saw from the shed, and cut the tree down. Her mother didn't think it was possible. But he managed it somehow with his right hand and the stump of his left arm. It took six hours. When the tree fell, it crushed the neighbor's greenhouse. That afternoon they found a note in their letter box. It was from the neighbor. It read:

> *I never liked that greenhouse and was going to*
> *knock it down this week.*
> *I'm so very sorry for you.*
> *Bill*

Then I see my Anna.

The rainy day.

The accident.

A car speeding away.

The back wheel of her bicycle still spinning.

I stopped the car and we sat at a picnic table and held hands. After a couple of hours a park official with long gray hair came over and told us we had to pay five dollars to picnic, so we left. It wasn't the money, but the atmosphere had changed. I started the car with my foot on the brake.

When we were back on the road, Hannah said she was hungry.

It had clouded over.

Fog wrapped the cliff in its thick coat.

Then it started to rain.

The swoosh of the windshield wipers was reassuring.

We turned inland at the first road.

The fog thinned out.

There were birds flying in the opposite direction—away from land. I couldn't think where they were going. Perhaps to a tall wet rock, far out at sea.

We stopped at a supermarket in Carmel for food. We held hands as the glass doors separated before us. I went for bread (the staple of my childhood). A few yards away

Hannah held up an apple. I nodded. She selected another. I held up the baguette. She nodded. I decided right then that I would never tell her about Anna.

The man at the deli counter wanted us to try the different things spread before him in shiny bowls. He gave us pieces of cheese and meat on toothpicks. He asked how long we were together.

"Forever," Hannah said.

At the checkout, Hannah noticed a box of kites. They were on sale. She bought two.

The cashier scrutinized the kites for a bar code.

"You should get one," Hannah said to her.

"I'm not into kites," the cashier replied.

"Then what are you into?" Hannah asked.

The cashier looked up. "Music," she said.

Hannah and I spent the night at a Buddhist retreat center in the mountains perched above Santa Cruz. I had heard about it from Sandy, my agent. She thought it might be a nice place for me. It was supposed to be very quiet, with large prayer wheels painted in bright colors. I stopped in Santa Cruz for gas. A man opposite the gas station was throwing bottles at passing cars and screaming. I hoped he wouldn't come over. I thought about it as we drove away. Hannah asked if I was okay.

"I'm fine," I said.

The key to our room was waiting for us. It was not late when we arrived, but the surrounding forest threw dark nets over all the buildings.

Hannah stayed in the shower for a very long time. The drops sounded like a heavy rain, which made me fall asleep.

When I awoke, Hannah was sitting at the edge of the bed drying her hair in a towel. It was hot in the room because the window was open. I sat up and wrapped her in the sheet. She turned to me, so I kissed her shoulders, then her neck, then her cheek, finally her lips.

My mouth lingered on hers; I tasted her. I felt for her tongue with mine. I felt the blood surging through my body. We pressed against one another.

Impossibly close.

She gripped my arms. Her nails tore into me. Soon we both were burning. Sweat pooled in the ridge of my back as I moved like a tide determined to crash against those ancient rocks.

Then—a moment before—inside, I kept very still. Our bodies moved of their own accord. Hannah's body was swallowing, digesting all that was mine to give. For those final moments, we existed seamlessly—all memory negated by a desire that both belonged to us and controlled us.

After, we kept very still, like the only two roots of the forest.

The sweat on our bodies dried.

We lay on our backs with our eyes open. I would like to have seen her eyes then. Mine were clear.

Finally she turned to me with great tenderness. She asked if I was hungry. I said I was, and so in the darkness we dressed and slipped out to the car.

The first restaurant we found was mostly empty, but the hostess said they were expecting a large party any minute. She suggested another place. So we left our car where it was and walked.

The sidewalk was very narrow and crowded with plants. It was completely dark and there were no streetlights. Hannah held my hand and led me through. We passed a dozen Craftsman houses from the 1930s. People were inside. We could see them. A couple sat in separate armchairs watching television. They laughed at the same time but did not look at one another. In another house, a small boy sat before a kitchen table. He was peeling an orange. In another, a woman undressed and then turned off the light. I pictured Edward Hopper across the street in a fedora gazing up from the shadows.

When we reached the other restaurant, there was a wedding party at the bar. A band played mediocre but recognizable music, and the guests sang the chorus. The groom was surrounded by his friends. They had loosened their neckties. Each drink had an umbrella in it.

Hannah ordered a cold glass of wine. Our waitress was in high school. She wore makeup. There were several pens tucked into her apron, and her jeans were rolled at the bottom.

We ate the same salad but from different plates. When an entrée of pasta arrived, we ate from the same plate. Then we just sat and held hands under the table.

"Do you think there's an afterlife?" Hannah said as I signed the check.

"I think we're in it," I said, and we left without anyone noticing.

We walked back to our car through the dark suburb. Most of the lights were out by then. I looked for the small boy, but he must have gone to bed.

The next day we continued driving south. We had wrapped some of the food from breakfast in paper towels. The rental car smelled like a hotel. We were wearing the same clothes as yesterday, but our hair smelled of Hannah's shampoo. Hannah wore shoes she said she hadn't liked for a long time. They were maroon-and-beige heels. I told her I liked them. I also told her how I had noticed her shoes a few moments after we collided. She looked down at her feet and moved them around.

Hannah was in a better mood. She hadn't mentioned

Jonathan, but whenever she thought about him, I could tell—she became quiet and still, like a statue. In Greek theater, the final breath of each tragic hero transforms the body to marble.

She told me about her life in Los Angeles, and then she wanted to know about New York. She was especially interested in Central Park. She'd heard there were parrots there. I told her the parrots were in Brooklyn.

I told her about my recent concert. The Central Park Conservancy had given me a "key" to the park. One of the benefits of possessing this key was a complimentary carriage ride. I recalled how I stood in line behind a man and his daughter. The little girl was about three years old. She had Cinderella clips in her hair. She was very excited that soon she would be riding in a carriage with her father. Her father bent down to her level to tell her things. Then he whispered something to her and she put her hands on his cheeks. Then I heard the girl remind her father that she was wearing underpants—that she wasn't young anymore.

The carriage attendant, who was watching a small television, hung up his cell phone, then stood up from his chair and informed everyone that the horse was very tired and would have to take a long break soon—so there would be only three more rides. The father and the girl were fourth in line. The girl tugged on her father's jacket and asked what the man had said. The father put his hand on her head but didn't say anything. The father looked around and sighed.

His daughter asked him to tell her more about the horse.

"Has Cinderella ever ridden on a horse? Or does she just ride in the carriage?"

And then suddenly two women in sweat suits who were third in line walked away. The father grabbed his daughter's hand and they moved up one space. The daughter asked if the horse was married and if it liked apples.

One of the women who had walked away told her friend that she was tired and wanted to go back to the hotel. Her friend laughed and they held each other's arms.

Hannah thought it was a nice story. Then we passed what I thought were sea lions. They were sea elephants, and Hannah made me stop so she could take photographs.

Every forty miles we would stop, either to walk around or smoke cigarettes. We even kissed a few times.

I had a concert in Phoenix in two days. I wondered if the city was named after the mythic bird that rose from the ashes. Hannah said it had to be.

When it got dark, I thought we could take blankets from the trunk and build a fire on the beach. I pulled into the parking lot of a convenience store and suggested that we walk across to the beach so that no one would know we were there. Hannah thought it was a clever idea, and I went inside to give the cashier twenty dollars. He seemed pleased with the arrangement.

The beach was much cooler than we'd imagined, but it felt good because, after parking, we kissed in the car for twenty minutes with the air-conditioning off. Hannah moved her neck when I kissed it, guiding my mouth into all the spaces she wanted to feel me.

I wasn't able to build a fire because the air was too damp. It got quite cold too. So we just lay under the blankets and held one another. I could feel her hair pressed against my neck. Her body fit perfectly with mine. She pulled her legs up. We lay very still, making outlines in the sand. In the background, waves pounded a scatter of rocks not far out.

I woke at dawn. It was still cold, but the air felt soft and fresh in my throat. Hannah was nowhere to be seen. I sat up and looked around. The beach was deserted. I wondered if she had gone back to the car to get warm. I decided to look for her, and then saw her erect body a few hundred yards away on the bluff. She was flying a kite.

When I reached her, the wind had blown back her hair. The wind was blowing so hard her eyes watered.

At first I thought I'd just sit and watch.

At her feet lay another kite, already assembled.

"That's your kite, Monsieur Bonnet," she said without looking at me.

I unfurled the line quickly, and Hannah told me to start on the beach and then run up the bluff in order to launch it. I tumble-ran down the bluff.

I held out the kite and hit the bluff running. My kite took easily.

It was exhilarating. I had not flown a kite in thirty years. The force pulling on me was more powerful than I could have imagined. But I was the one who held on. I was not captive but captor.

We flew our kites for most of the morning, occasionally glancing at one another.

Then Hannah let her kite go.

It quickly rose, twisting brilliantly against the climbing sun.

Allez, I thought.

And my fingers released the strings of my own kite.

The force we had held fast against our bodies abruptly ceased.

The kites tore through the heavens. They were soon nothing more than two specks of color. And then both disappeared from our sight. Even though we knew they were out there, there was no way to ever bring them back.

Six months later I played for one night only in Paris. Instead of staying at the hotel, I rented a car and drove home to Noyant. I arrived about six o'clock in the morning. There were birds everywhere and the roads were empty. I sat with the baker in his small cake shop. I told him the whole story of how I collided with Hannah at a hotel in California. I wanted to explain why I hadn't been in touch for several months and also to confess how happiness still felt remote—as though I were watching it happen to someone else. It was a cool morning. Children trudged to school, not completely awake. The sky outside was rubbed gray. Clouds passed like open hands. The sky would soon be full of falling drops. The baker sat with me and dried his hands on his apron. His wife joined him from the back. I could smell fresh mushrooms. The radio was on.

The baker gathered my hands in his and told me how glad he was I hadn't been in touch—and that I must promise to stop sending stones. I suddenly felt very selfish and vain. I shrank from him. I pulled my hands away.

But then he said: "Bruno—we lost a daughter—we don't want to lose a son."

"That is what you would have been to us," his wife said.

"That is what you have become to us," the baker said and took his wife's hand.

"Send postcards from now on," he said. "No more stones, eh?"

Before I went to see my parents, the baker's wife suggested that when Hannah comes to France, perhaps I might introduce them to her. Perhaps they might make her a cake and serve it to her in the shop with a bowl of steaming coffee—that we might just be four people sitting down to a small meal in the evening.

ALMOST A YEAR AFTER I met Hannah, the birdman
died. His obituary was one of the longest ever printed
in the *Los Angeles Times*. His life was unlike any of the
rumors. There was a candlelight vigil in the park attended
by thousands of people. Instead of birds, there were heli-
copters.

But I was far away in the middle of France, back in Noyant
at the shop eating cakes with an old man and his wife. Children peered in at us through misty windows. They rubbed
their mittens on the glass and talked loudly. They were excited because it was the first afternoon that bicycles would
be sold against the church wall.

It was snowing hard. The baker was very round and his
apron fit snugly about his middle. He went into the kitchen
and then quickly reappeared with a tray of pastry scraps.
The children saw him coming and stood by the door. Then
we saw arms reaching for the tray and heard a chorus of
"*Merci, Monsieur.*" When he came back in, there were
snowflakes on his shoulders.

"They expect it now." He shrugged. "I've been feeding
them since they were the size of baguettes."

The baker's wife laughed.

"They call him the children's baker," she said.

The baker went behind the counter and poured himself a small glass of brandy.

He looked at Hannah for a long time.

Then he walked over and kissed the top of her head.

The baker's wife stared out through the window—at the world that lay beyond it and the mysterious place beyond that.

When it started to get dark, Hannah and I left the shop. Bicycles were being wheeled home in the snow. Old women left bricks of cake on one another's doorsteps. The butcher was dressed up like Santa Claus.

Children peered out into the night from upstairs windows. And for several kilometers Hannah and I waded through snowy fields, past old gates and fallen trees, laughing and calling out as our bodies disappeared from view.

The shadows remained.

Gifts from the fallen, not lessening our happiness but guiding it, deepening it, and filling us with the passion we would need to sustain our love in the coming days.

A gentle reminder that what we have is already lost.

Tiger, Tiger

WHEN I FIRST SAW Jennifer, I thought she was dead. She was lying facedown on the couch. The curtains were not drawn. Her naked body soaked up the falling moonlight and her back glowed.

Jennifer was Brian's mother. When he frantically turned her over, she moaned. Then her arm flew back, viciously but at nothing. Brian told me to call 911, but Jennifer screamed at him not to. Brian switched on a lamp. He kept his distance and said, "Mom, Mom." Then he asked where Dad was. She moaned again. Neither of us knew what to do.

Brian fetched a bathrobe and laid it across her back. She sat up, then pulled it around herself weakly. The robe was too big and gaped in several places. One of her breasts was visible. I know Brian could see it. It was like an old ashen bird. I made coffee without asking. There was cake in the refrigerator. It said "Tate's Bakery" on the box. I cut the string. With the same knife I cut three equal pieces. We ate and drank in silence. Jennifer swallowed each forkful quietly; my yoga instructor would have called her mindful. She shook her head from side to side. Then Brian and I watched as Jennifer buried her face in her hands as though she were watching a slide show of her life projected across her palms.

On the carpet next to Jennifer's clothes were several brochures for new cars. There was also a wedding band and a glass of something that had been knocked over. The contents of the glass had dried into the carpet and looked like a map of Italy.

We sat in silence; a forced intimacy, like three strangers sheltering under a doorway in pouring rain.

I remembered a childhood dream that went like this: The night before something exciting, such as going on vacation or a birthday party, I would dream of accidentally sleeping through the whole thing. In the dream I would believe I had missed everything—that the event was over; it had taken place without me.

Brian and I had been together for eighteen months when his parents decided they wanted to meet me. I was indifferent. I was thirty-four and settled in a practice with several other doctors. I didn't care about living up to their expectations. I got tired of all that after I entered medical school and started clumsily slicing my way through cadavers. I come into contact with life and death on a daily basis, but not through ailing retirees battling heart disease and lamenting their crumbling bones but through children, who are never to blame for anything that happens to them. I wanted to be a pediatrician from the start.

Countless children have waited outside my office with my secretary, Lauren, a southern redhead with flawless skin. I explain to parents the problem, the procedure, and the risk—in that order. The lone parent never cries, but couples do, even if the prognosis is positive. As they console one another, I often think of the little head swiveling around the waiting room, reading a book about boats, or looking at a plant, or staring at Lauren, unaware of the long and often arduous journey that some force in the universe has chosen for them.

It doesn't do children any good to see their parents upset, and so I sometimes let the child take Lauren out for ice cream.

Several years ago, Brian's parents bought a summerhouse in Hampton Bays. I personally don't like Long Island. It's overpopulated and people find safety through excess. The goal of life seems to revolve around ownership and luxury—just as it did for the English four hundred years ago. It's everything my parents were against in the 1960s. Either America has changed significantly in the last decade or overeducation has left me cynical. So many revere a vehicle like the Hummer and other glorified farm equipment while spending their lives in ignorance of how their own organs work. We plead with God to spare us from disease, while consciously filling our bodies with toxins.

I don't much like the Hamptons either. In the years I have been going out there, it's become a police state—and the police are paid handsomely for what amounts to guarding the estates of a few homegrown aristocrats.

Perhaps you wouldn't think my views extreme if I explained that my parents are from Oregon. I grew up wandering misty fields and sketching cows. My mother knitted clothes and my father built my one and only dollhouse in his workshop. My town is staunchly Democratic and well known as a haven for lesbians—imagine coffee shops and furniture stores run by tattooed women who bake upside-down cake for one another.

They both visited once. My mother feels abandoned by me, her only child. But then she was always strange—somehow detached at key moments. When I was in high school, I put it down to menopause, but now I think it's something that's been long-standing since childhood. My father would never say anything critical to her—he would just rub his chin or rub her hand. My father spent his life rubbing things, like Aladdin.

Of course, my parents didn't understand the Hamptons when they visited, the summer before I met Brian. Especially my father, who became flustered when we were stopped at a beach checkpoint and told we had to pay the town a fee in order to park at the ocean. My father told the teenage attendant that the Town of Southampton was no better than the mafia. But then people behind us started honking. Over dinner at a lobster shack close to where the fishing boats dock, my father said we would have been better off under the British. My mother said that if the British had retained the colonies, the only difference would be that everyone would have bad teeth. The waitress overheard and laughed. She gave my father a beer on the house and told him to cheer up.

On the way back to the city my father looked strangely sad. I think he was going through something painful that he couldn't talk to my mother about. I wish I'd asked. He died last year.

After that long visit, the novelty of upper-middle-class New York life wore off and I appreciated the city for what it was, an indifferent, throbbing pulse with an infinite number of chances to reinvent yourself.

It was sweet of Alan and Jennifer, Brian's parents, to say I was the first of their son's girlfriends to be asked out to their summerhouse in Hampton Bays. But they quickly ruined it by saying they only wanted to meet the ones he was serious about—as though the less serious ones were meaningless. Alan and Jennifer referred often to their summerhouse when they left messages on Brian's machine, which led me to suspect they'd grown up poor. Actually they hadn't. Jennifer was the daughter of a real estate husband-and-wife team from Garden City. Alan was the son of a Jewish tailor from the Lower East Side who knew how to save money and collect secrets while he measured inseams. Brian said his grandfather's knowledge of clients' personal lives helped get Alan into a private school where Jews were not particularly welcomed. When Alan's father died, his few remaining clients on Park Avenue breathed a sigh of relief.

Brian has a younger sister, Martha. I met her once at a concert in Irving Plaza. Perhaps because she isn't pretty, she had decided to be ironic and make her body the canvas for a series of strange tattoos, one of which is an artichoke.

Brian's mother, Jennifer, was once physically beautiful. In the photographs which dotted the living room of their Hampton Bays summer home, she looked perpetually overjoyed—her mouth painted and open like a rose moving its petals.

The night Brian and I arrived in Hampton Bays we kissed in the car before going in. It's something we do. We are always kissing. Brian stopped abruptly when he suddenly noticed the house was in darkness.

"That's strange," Brian said. "There are no lights on." I sensed something was terribly wrong.

Jennifer's eyes were so puffy I felt awkward looking at her. I quietly asked Brian if he wanted me to examine them.

He said they always puffed up when she was upset, but he'd never seen them like this.

Alan, Jennifer's husband, had walked out that afternoon. He returned from his tennis match and started packing a suitcase. A woman in a convertible picked him up. She waited at the end of the driveway with the engine turning over. He said he wasn't coming back. He said Ken, their lawyer, would sort out the arrangements. Jennifer chased after the car and threw her shoes at it. Then she walked home. They had been married for thirty-four years. They were married the year I was born.

Brian's father was fifty-seven years old when he left Jennifer. Alan's father, the Jewish tailor, was fifty-seven when he died of a coronary thrombosis. It was a psychoanalytical cliché, but I kept quiet and said nothing to Brian—even intelligent people go nuts around their parents.

I asked Brian again if he wanted me to examine his mother and he said no—that they had a close family friend, a Dr. Felixson, that his mother trusted and who was at his summerhouse in Southampton. I couldn't hide my disappointment. "Let's just get through tonight," he said. "You should meet this guy anyway—he wrote a book back in the seventies on pediatrics or something."

"Really," I said.

As I waited outside in the darkness for the doctor, Brian came out with a copy of Dr. Felixson's book, *The Silence*

After Childhood. It was an odd title. I said I would read it. Then Brian told me he'd known about his father's affair. Apparently, Alan had confessed over dinner several months ago. Jennifer had been visiting her family in Florida. Brian thought I would be angry with him for not telling me. But I wasn't.

"What man could resist the opportunity to live twice?" Brian said his father had pleaded. He perceived his son's silence as reluctant approval, but in truth, Brian was disappointed. He finally had to admit his father's cowardice. The marriage to his mother had never been harmonious, but he'd stayed in it. Brian said that if his father wasn't such a coward, he would have hurt Jennifer thirty years ago, instead of hurting her *and* humiliating her after three wasted decades.

"But then Martha wouldn't have been born," I said. Brian was silent for a moment. I thought he was mad at me, but then he said that regardless of his sister, his father had stolen his mother's life.

"But Jennifer let him steal it," I added.

Brian nodded. I think he appreciated my frankness, but I shouldn't have said it then.

The doctor arrived in an old station wagon. A kayak was tied on the roof. He got out and waved. Then he opened the trunk and reached for his bag.

He was a tall, thin man who looked as though he could

have been a nineteenth-century Midwestern farmer. His unkempt white hair and strange side-to-side walk gave him the appearance of being drunk. He was born and raised in Stockholm. He'd moved to New York in the 1970s. He wasn't married.

"Brian, my boy, sorry to see you under these circumstances, but we'll sort this out together," Dr. Felixson said quietly. He walked up to me and put his hand on my shoulder. Then he said, "What madness has driven you to retrieve a copy of that book you're holding?"

Before disappearing inside, he turned around and said, "Brian tells me you both went to Stockholm, yes?"

"Yes," I said. "It was beautiful, but it didn't snow."

"Times change, I suppose," he said.

One night, maybe our third date. Brian and I lying in bed. The room sketched by moonlight. The street outside in a deep sleep. Snowing and we didn't even know.

Brian said he and his sister had trembled with fear at his parents' arguments. "They screeched like birds," he said.

Brian said he would never get married. I hesitated. Years of adolescent sleepovers had engraved images of the perfect day. In truth, I hadn't thought about marriage for years.

Brian sensed my fear. He reached for my hand under the blanket. I gave it to him. He was no coward—maybe that was worth a thousand perfect wedding days.

Brian believed that marriage often gives one party the

license to behave intolerably without the fear of being abandoned because the state must oversee any separation. He said that with many couples he knew, either the husband or the wife had waited until they were married to really hang out their dirty washing. He believed that marriage was an outdated concept, like circumcision in gentiles.

"But not in Jews?" I said.

"It's more complicated than that," he said, but in a kind way, as if to say I had a point too.

The next day we went to McCarren Park and built a snowman. A young Hispanic boy helped us with the finishing touches. The boy held my hand for a while. Then he said Brian and I should get married. Brian looked at me and laughed, then asked him if he'd settle for a cup of hot chocolate at the Greenpoint Café. The boy said he would. I had wanted Brian all to myself but loved how he was so inclusive. I suggested the boy call his mother and tell her where he was. I gave him my cell phone. Later that night, I noticed there was no new number on my call list. The boy had just held the phone to his ear and talked.

That was one of the nicest days I've ever had with anyone. Later we went to a fondue restaurant and then stayed up all night drinking and listening to Getz and Gilberto. I remember dancing. Brian watched.

A week later when the snow melted, we decided to go to Sweden for a long weekend. It cost more than we thought because you forget to include things like car service to the airport and then the money you happily waste in duty-free. We were both in graduate school, so it took us a year to pay the trip off. I remember we held hands on the flight. You can't put a price on the rituals of love, because you never know what will happen next. I suppose fear is part of the excitement and we can't have one without the other.

Dr. Felixson examined Jennifer in private. We heard her crying. Then we heard Dr. Felixson's voice. It sounded like he was talking to Brian's father on the phone. Before he left, he said that we should call him if we had any questions and that, with any luck, we'd all live through this. I was too tired to get one of my cards from the car, and so I said I would send him an e-mail. Of course, I never did.

Soon after Dr. Felixson left the house, his sedative began to pull Jennifer out to sleep like a tug silently towing a ship out to sea. She mumbled that if Alan showed up or called back, to tell him she was dead. I nodded.

Then she lay down on the couch, and the sedative pulled her under so violently that she began to snore a few moments after closing her eyes.

I was surprised I understood why Jennifer couldn't go into the bedroom and lie down. I covered her up with another blanket. Body temperature drops at night.

Brian came over and put his arm around me. He turned off the lamp and kissed me. Then suddenly I felt strange.

I pulled away.

He sat there for a moment.

Then he kissed my forehead and went outside. I heard him drive away. He wasn't mad, because we understand one another——like two maps pressed together in a book.

It was either the semidarkness of the room or the smell of late summer pushing at the screens——or even the fabric of the couch on my bare legs. All these things in that moment seemed like props arranged by my memory to suddenly transport me to a moment which had long passed.

The exactitude of feeling two years old flickered inside me. I kept very still. I felt like primitive man having inadvertently made fire and wishing, more than anything, to keep it burning just a few moments longer.

It's as if my two-year-old self had been living inside me like the second smallest piece in a set of Russian dolls. It now rose to the surface of my consciousness, and I felt with absolute clarity how it felt to be two years old on one particular day in the 1970s.

My parents had taken me to the park across the street from our house because it was my birthday. There was a party; other children came. The other children weren't my friends; they were just other children. My parents were my best friends, which was why it was so hurtful when they reproached me.

My feet suddenly rose off the floor, pulled up into my

shrinking body. I could feel the scabs on my knees like small islands. I pushed my tongue into the spaces where I had no teeth. Dry birthday cake. Juice with crumbs in it. Mild nausea. I pictured the candles, but the feeling was stronger than anything I could visually recall. It was as though I were there but without my eyes or my sense of touch. I remember running through tall grass. I can feel it brushing against my legs like long, thin arms. The other children's high-pitched cries. Presents lowered from large, foreign hands.

The end of the party. I didn't want to go home. I was frustrated that everyone was separating. I wanted the day to rewind itself. Then I remember chasing a boy. My parents calling me. His parents watching us, grinning, encouraging us. He falls, turns over laughing. I'm laughing too. I come upon him. I take his arm and bite into it. Blood appears from nowhere and spreads on his skin. He looks at his arm. He screams and parents scramble. He is scooped up like a bug. I want to say that I am a tiger and tigers bite. I want to remind them I can be a tiger. His face turns red as he is pulled up into the nest of his mother's arms. I sense the tone of crying change from shock to something else. He lifts his arm. His mother kisses it. She rocks him. His father stands erect, on guard, looking around, helpless, pathetic.

I am rooted to the spot by fear. Then suddenly my diaper is yanked down. I recoil but am held in place as my mother's hand clips my bottom. The crack of her hand against my flesh. My little body making forward jerks with each smack. My disgruntled face, my curling lip like a glistening crimson wave.

My eyes are open, but I am almost unconscious with shock and humiliation.

I can feel wind on the exposed flesh of my bottom. My mother walks away. I am burning with emotions too great for my small body. I am undressed in public. There are spots of blood on the grass. People gather around and peer down at me sadly.

I overhear a woman ask if I am a boy or a girl.

I am too scared to pull my diaper up.

My mother has walked away.

My father carries me across the field toward our house. As soon as he pulled my diaper up, I defecated into it. He rubbed my head. My mother stayed at the park with her arms crossed. She had taken off her fancy shoes.

My father said: "You cannot bite—biting is wrong." But there was no passion in his voice. Then we reached the house.

He put me in their bedroom. He closed the blinds, but ribs of light fell through and settled upon the floor as though I were in the stomach of some celestial being. My father stripped me down to my diaper. It was full of feces. I was too afraid to cry. I wondered if I would be killed without knowing what death was. The fabric of the chair stuck to my tiny, fleshy legs. It was my birthday. I was two. Sweat had dried across my body like a veil.

Later, a plate of birthday cake was left outside the door.

"What if she's sleeping?" my father whispered. "She won't be," my mother snapped.

I didn't want the cake. I wanted my mother to forget herself and remember me. Eventually they brought the cake into the room. I ate it and cried and sat between them and repeated over and over mechanically that biting was wrong. But deep down I still loved the boy and would have bitten him again and again, forever. And he knew I loved him. And it was pure and spontaneous.

And so I became a pediatrician. I wanted to be a hand that's lowered to souls dangling off the cliff in darkness.

About two years after Brian and I found Jennifer on the couch in Hampton Bays, I finished Dr. Felixson's *The Silence After Childhood*. I read it in one sitting. It was 3 AM on Monday morning. I picked up the phone and called Brian.

"I have just read Dr. Felixson's book."

There was silence and then Brian said:

"See what I told you?"

"Do you want to come over?" I said.

"Don't you have work in a few hours?"

"Jesus, Brian."

"Okay, okay—I'll bring my clothes for tomorrow."

I was trembling. Dr. Felixson's insights had set off small

earthquakes in my body. They were spreading to my memory like soft, warm hands eager to unearth buried things.

When Brian arrived, I sat him down, kissed him, thanked him for coming over, and handed him a glass of whiskey. I opened the book randomly and read a passage.

"Listen to this," I said.

> *To children, parents can seem like blocks of wood—or at best, sad creatures that seem always on the verge of not loving them. Later, we adults learn that our parents are consumed with neuroses they've manifested as seemingly real problems to draw the spotlight away from a more painful reality....*

I closed the book and opened it to another page. Brian leaned forward.

> *There's no going back to childhood unless you're somehow tethered to it and can feel the weight of it against your body like a kite pulling at you from its invisible world; then you will understand everything through feeling, and the world will be at once tender and brutal and you'll have no way of knowing which on any given day. And you'll love everyone deeply but learn not to trust anyone....*

"Wow," Brian said. "Dr. Felixson wrote that?"

"I thought you'd read this?"

He looked up. "It's been in our house for so long. I always meant to," he said.

I turned several pages and let my eyes fall into a paragraph:

> *Childhood is terrifying because adults make children feel as though they are incomplete, as if they know nothing, when a child's instinct tells her she knows everything. But then perhaps the most damaging crimes in a society are committed by most of its citizens and perpetuated unknowingly. . . .*

Jennifer is now living in Florida. She is writing her memoirs. She is seeing someone. He's *Italian* Italian, she says, and he's apparently related to Tony Bennett and has the family voice. Alan lives year-round in Hampton Bays. His relationship fell apart a few months after he left Jennifer. He tells Brian he's "playing the field." He's started wearing cologne. I often wonder if Jennifer and Alan were as close as Brian and I are.

I know Brian has wondered if I've thought about whether he would leave me in the same way. But Brian is not like his father. Brian is a beautiful child, but he's not childish. Children are the closest we have to wisdom, and they become adults the moment that final drop of everything mysterious is strained from them. I think it happens quietly to every one of us—like crossing a state line when you're asleep.

Brian and I may part one day, but it's not really parting— you can't undo what's done. The worst wouldn't be so bad— just the future unknown. Though I would carry a version of him inside me. But isn't every future unwritten? The idea of fate is really only a matter of genetics now. But what's interesting is how so many significant events in my life have come from seemingly random things. Freedom is the most exciting of life's terrors:

I'd decided on whim to walk into a bookstore. There was Brian.

I wonder if I had never met Brian, what I would have thought about all the times I've thought about him. Would my head have been empty of thoughts? Would it have been similar to sleep? Or would other thoughts have been there? Where are those thoughts now, and what would they have been about?

I've thought about these sorts of things since I began editing the unpublished writings of Dr. Felixson. A few days after finishing *The Silence After Childhood*, I tried to call him. A woman renting his old surgery space said he'd died.

I had more than forty pages of questions.

Unbeknownst to Brian, Jennifer had come into possession of some of Dr. Felixson's journals. I discovered this when I called her in Florida. I wanted to find out more about his life. There was singing in the background. Jennifer giggled and asked if I could hear it. I explained the effect Dr. Felixson's book was having on my life. She asked if Brian was there. He was. She asked to speak to him. She then explained to her son how she and the doctor had experienced a brief affair several years before Alan left her. The marriage had never been the same after. Brian was so shocked he hung up. Jennifer immediately called back and said she would have spared him, but she wanted to explain why she had only some of Dr. Felixson's journals. In his will, Dr. Felixson had left Jennifer the journals covering the period of their togetherness.

In a gesture of kindness and courage, Jennifer sent them all to me from Florida via UPS. She said that what little had been written about her was nothing compared with the notes he'd made on his patients and his general everyday thoughts.

"He writes about everyday things like clouds," she said.

She was adamant that they be in the hands of another doctor. I felt truly honored.

When they arrived, I wrote back to Jennifer, asking if she had loved Dr. Felixson and why the affair had ended after only a few weeks. She wrote back almost immediately. She said Blix Felixson was the only man she had ever met who could love unconditionally without having to be loved back. She said it was unnerving because he was never disappointed by anything.

Or he was disappointed by everything. But I didn't suggest this. I had learned my lesson.

December 23rd, 1977

For infants, discomfort in any measure is hopefully met with physical and emotional contact with a parent or caregiver. Could it be then, in the silence and confusion after we falsely perceive childhood has ended, that our experience of discomfort is met with an instinct to seek solace through the same end? An emotional reassurance from another human being bound up with physical embrace? So then, in adulthood, could it be possible that we spend the majority of our lives looking for comfort from strangers?

Adult fears are idealized to the point where they have become too big to fit through the hole they originally came through.

People's expectations of coupling
may be too grand, and thus disappointment, loneliness, and often pain are
the inevitable adjuncts of something
we thought would be the ultimate answer (an emotional cure-all) to our
ongoing fears. Many people who feel
an emotional emptiness when alone for
long periods look to marriage the way
someone financially poor views winning
a jackpot.

All wars are the external realiza-
tion of our internal battles. Humans
must learn not to blame each other
for being afraid, disappointed, or in
pain. We perhaps might learn to view
those we have special feelings toward
as being our companions rather than
our saviors, companions on the journey
back to childhood. But there is nothing to find. We must only unravel. And
in the meantime--lower our expectations of each other (and ourselves!) in
order to "love" more deeply and more
humanly.

It is almost dark now. I can hear
rain on the window, but I cannot see
it. A car drives past. I wonder who is
in it.

I wonder what life would be like
if I now were married. Perhaps the
smell of cake would fill the house. I
think of Mother and Father. I remember
launching my model aeroplanes off the
hill at Skansen. Visiting my father's
office in Stockholm in the bright noon
sun. I remember my father's face. My
mother's face. If only I could speak
to them now. It would be a different story altogether. I would forgive
them.

Dr. Felixson died alone and was not discovered for
several days. The *Southampton Press* reported that a
doctor of many disciplines who was of some note, had
passed away from causes unknown at his Shinnecock
Hills cottage, and was discovered by a landscaping crew
who called local police when they saw an elderly man
through an open window lying on the floor, apparently
unconscious.

July 7th, 1977

It's true the people we meet shape us. But the people we don't meet shape us also, often more because we have imagined them so vividly.

There are people we yearn for but never seem to meet. Every adult yearns for some stranger, but it is really childhood we miss. We are yearning for that which has been stolen from us by what we have become.

Brian is something in the universe and I am something in the universe, and our real names are not sounds or marks on a page but bodies. We meet and then we recede.

We can never truly be one sea, though we are both water.

June 21st, 1978

We are not at home in the world because we imagine it is as we have become, full of nothing but yearning and forgetting and hoping for something so raw we can't describe it. We think

```
of the world as the place of begin-
nings and ends, and we forget the in-
between, and even how to inhabit our
own bodies. And then in adulthood, we
sit and wonder why we feel so lost.
```

It is Sunday afternoon and Brian and I are driving out to Hampton Bays to see Alan. We've been together almost four years. I have been editing the journals of Dr. Felixson. They will be published the year after next by a man I think Dr. Felixson would have admired. I have my own practice now, but eventually I'd like to teach. I have had an article published on Dr. Felixson's methods in pediatric psychology in the *New England Journal of Medicine*. His first book, *The Silence After Childhood*, is being reissued next year by a publisher based in Berlin. Since my article was published, I have received thirty-four letters from doctors across the world.

Brian sometimes tells me anecdotes about when Dr. Felixson examined him as a child. I love these and write them down.

Brian and I have also decided to live together, but we're never getting married.

November 17th, 1980

Today, a woman touched my sleeve
in the supermarket as I was trying to
pick out good strawberries. She asked
if I was the children's doctor from
Germany. I corrected her and explained
that Sweden is much, much colder in
some ways but not in others. She asked
me if I had a moment, and I said of
course, though I thought to myself,
it is an interesting thing to say because one's life is nothing more than
a string of moments. Each life is like
a string of pearls.

This woman wanted to know why her
four-year-old son, when she met him at
school, had given his macaroni drawing to another boy's mother and not to
her. She said she didn't speak to her
son all the way home and even cried.
Then she said he cried and locked himself in his bedroom. She was worried
that her son didn't love her--other-
wise why would he give his drawing to
some other child's mother?

I laughed a little and ate one of
the strawberries I was holding. Is
that all? I said. She nodded. Well,
I explained, you are worrying about
the wrong person. I explained that the
reason her son had given the drawing
to another mother was because he loved
her, his own mother, with such blind,
unprecedented devotion, that naturally
he felt sorry for every other woman
in the world, whom he did not love so
vehemently.

Then of all things, the woman
started to cry. She touched my sleeve
again and said, Thank you, Doctor.
She said she was going to buy him a
toy to make up for it--but I said to
her, Perhaps, Madame, instead of buying a toy, you should simply go home,
find your son and remind him of the
event, and tell him that you love him
with equal devotion, and that you will
never again question his judgment when
it comes to how he expresses his love
for his mother.

When I thought more about the en-

counter on the way home, I found myself
getting depressed. So when I got home,
I put my robe on and gave my strawberries to the birds. What a beautiful
child that woman has, I thought. What
a genius boy, and what a hard life he
has ahead of him in this world where
beauty is categorized and natural love
is negated by flattery.

Toys

*Toys are the props by which children share
their fears, their hopes, their disappointments, and
their victories with the outside world.*

*The toys parents choose for their children will
set the boundaries of their play (fantasy). A heavily
representational toy may limit the child's play to
those aspects the child associates with the context.
For example, a toy based on a television character
will determine the way the child plays with the toy
and thus limit the fantasy.*

*Toys that are not representative of some third
party (the child and the toy are the first and second
party) allow children to develop and explore their own*

fantasies with less distortion. However, if your child seems unhappy at the idea of playing with pieces of wood or wool shapes, then introduce a few props from nature (leaves from a park or hard vegetables such as pumpkins or potatoes). These will allow your child to set his fantasy in the natural world.

Present your child with a cooking pot, and he will pretend to cook. Give your child a gun, and he will pretend to shoot. It's an easy choice for the thinking parent (unless the child is born into ancient Spartan culture!).

For a child, asking someone to play *is an act of trust. And trust helps build love. For the child is eager (through toys) to share her private world with you, and to express through play (with toys as props) what she cannot express through language—either because she doesn't inherently trust language (and why should she?—see Chapter 2, "Everything Is a Metaphor") or because she doesn't yet possess the skills to express herself clearly through the speaking circuit.*

Play to a child's emotional development is like food to physical development. Play is a tool for loving. Even the most healthy adult relationships I have studied rely heavily on forms of play.

CONVERSATION WITH FOUR-YEAR-OLD DOROTHY

Dr. Felixson:	*Why are toys so important?*
Dorothy:	*They are important for kids.*
Dr. Felixson:	*Why is that?*
Dorothy:	*Because kids like to play.*
Dr. Felixson:	*Hmm. I wonder why they like to play?*
Dorothy:	*I don't know.*
Dr. Felixson:	*I wonder why kids want to play with grown-ups?*
Dorothy:	*Maybe because they like grown-ups so much?*

Astonishing, isn't it? Dorothy knows she is being questioned, and like most children, she wants to please. She is eager to talk, but perhaps a more effective way to understand children is to do it on their own terms. If I were to play with Dorothy (toys of her choosing) and then study that play, I might understand Dorothy's world more clearly. To question Dorothy as though she were a simple adult as I did above is a great failing on my part. And since writing this, I have changed the way I explore children's perception. To experience an apple, don't eat the apple—become the seed.

PAGES 221–223, CHAPTER 8, *THE IMPORTANCE OF*
TOYS BY DR. BLIX FELIXSON, GREENPOINT PAPER-
BACKS, NEW YORK, 1972.

Driving through Riverhead, Brian asks me to unwrap a
sandwich we picked up at Greenpoint Café for our trip. He
watches me unfold the paper and reaches out to take a half.
I slap his hand.

"No," I say. "I want us to share the same half."

Trivial secrets and unspoken pacts keep us going.

We're driving through East Quogue. The road has
thinned to a gray strip that slips through a forest. I think of
the forest as my childhood.

Brian touches the back of my neck. My concentration
breaks like a wave against the shore.

"Remember the champagne glasses?" he says.

I think of the two delicate champagne flutes we left in
the Adirondack Mountains a few weeks ago. Brian and I
were hiking. There are forests so thick it's like perpetual
night—or the subconscious, Brian remarked. The air is thin
and crisp. At night, we fell asleep with wood smoke in our
hair.

After hiking nine miles up into the white breath of a
mountain, we were truly invisible to one world but in the
palm of another. Brian heard a river. We followed the sound
and then spotted a rock in the middle, large and flat enough

for our bodies to sit on comfortably. It had been raining, but it's amazing how quickly the sun dries the earth after it has been washed.

Brian and I lay our bodies on the rock. I closed my eyes. The sound of water was deafening. Brian unwrapped a bottle of champagne and two wineglasses from several T-shirts. I was surprised he would bring such things up into the woods. Then he explained. It was the anniversary of our first date. I told him it wasn't but that I'd help him drink the champagne to lighten his load.

We lay on our backs. The sun in and out of clouds. The silence of the sky intimidating. A landscape of thought.

Then Brian laughed and told me I was right. It wasn't our anniversary. I felt then he was somehow disappointed and so told him that every moment with him is a small anniversary. I don't know what it meant. It just came to me.

We kissed, and that led to us making love. It was sweet and slow. My foot trailed in the water like a rudder.

After, Brian pulled a towel from his rucksack and put it under our heads.

When I awoke, Brian was gazing down off the side of the rock into a deep pool. His bare back was a field of bronze muscle. I had forgotten his male strength. It was late afternoon. The sky had bruised. There was a wind and the trees shook. Wind is the strangest thing. The word describes a phenomenon.

I reached for Brian. I lay my palm on his back. He pointed to the pool beneath the rock. The scent of pine was overwhelming.

While I was sleeping, the champagne glasses had rolled off the bags and fallen into the rock pool below. By some miracle they had fallen upright. The river gushed through the rocks and then into the pool where the glasses stood. Each glass held the weight of an entire river without knowing where it came from and how much was left.

Suddenly, in the car just a few miles from Alan's house in Hampton Bays, I reach for Brian's arm. I dip my head and bite into it. I feel my teeth clamp his warm flesh. He shouts, then screams when I won't let go. The car runs off the road into the woods. There is thumping from underneath. Brian yanks his arm back, still screaming. The front wheels come to rest in a tangle of leaves and branches. I can taste Brian's salty blood in my mouth.

Brian looks at me and then incredulously at his arm. It bears the perfect indentation of my mouth, but the line is blurred by shallow bleeding.

Brian's eyes are full and swirling.

We breathe heavily, as though inhaling one another. Then it starts to rain. Nothing but the sound of drops falling. The rear lights of passing cars break into blood-red bloom through the rain-spattered windshield.

My eyes like leaves, long and wet.

Alan has baked lasagna. He arranges the chairs so that we sit close, so that in the end, as light dims and the curtain falls on another small day, we won't lose sight of each other's eyes, even if everything in-between has been lost or fell away one cloudy afternoon to the sound of passing traffic.

The Missing Statues

ONE BRIGHT WEDNESDAY MORNING in Rome, a young American diplomat collapsed onto a bench at the edge of St. Peter's Square.

There, he began to sob.

An old room in his heart had opened because of something he'd seen.

Soon he was weeping so loudly that a young Polish priest parking a yellow Vespa felt inclined to do something. The priest silently placed himself on the bench next to the man.

A dog with gray whiskers limped past and then lay on its side in the shade. Men leaned on their brooms and talked in twos and threes. The priest reached his arm around the man and squeezed his shoulder dutifully. The young diplomat turned his body to the priest and wept into his cloth. The fabric carried a faint odor of wood smoke. An old woman in black nodded past, fingering her rosary and muttering something too quiet to hear.

By the time Max stopped crying, the priest had pictured the place where he was supposed to be. He imagined the empty seat at the table. The untouched glass of water. The heavy sagging curtains and the smell of polish. The meeting would be well under way. He considered the idea that he was always where he was supposed to be, even when he wasn't.

"You're okay now?" the priest asked. His Polish accent clipped at the English words like carefully held scissors.

"I'm so embarrassed," Max said.

Then Max pointed to the row of statues standing along the edge of St. Peter's Square.

The priest looked up.

"Well, they're beautiful—oh, but look, there is a statue missing," the priest exclaimed. "How extraordinary."

The priest turned to Max.

"Why would a missing statue upset you, Signor Americano—you didn't steal it, did you?"

Max shook his head. "Something from my childhood."

"I've always believed that the future is hung with keys that unlock our true feelings about some past event," the priest said.

"Isn't everything something from childhood?" the priest continued. "A scribble that was never hung, an unkind word before bed, a forgotten birthday—"

"Yes, but it doesn't have to be so negative, Father," Max interrupted. "There are moments of salvation too, aren't there?"

"If there aren't," the priest said, "then God has wasted my life."

The two men sat without talking as if they were old friends. The priest hummed a few notes from a Chopin nocturne and counted clouds.

Then a bird landed in the space where the divine being had once stood—where its eyes had once fallen upon the people who milled about the square, eating sandwiches, taking photographs, feeding babies, birds, and the occasional vagrant who wandered in quietly from the river.

The priest looked at Max and pointed up at the statues again. "They should all be missing," he joked, but then wasn't sure if the man beside him understood what he meant.

Max blew his nose and brushed the hair from his face.

"Please forgive me," Max said. "You're very kind, but really I'm fine now—*grazie mille*."

The Polish man sitting next to him had entered the priesthood after volunteering as a children's counselor in the poorest area of Warsaw. He couldn't believe what he saw. He quickly climbed the ranks and was skilled at negotiating the bureaucracy that plagues all men of action. Through his close work with young, troubled children, the priest understood the reluctance of men to share their troubles.

"You can tell me anything," the priest said. "I don't just pray—I give advice too."

Max smiled.

"I simply want to know why a missing statue has reduced a young American businessman to tears," the priest said.

The priest's hair was as yellow as hay. It naturally slanted to one side. He was handsome, and Max thought it a shame he would never marry.

"Just a long-ago story I once heard," Max said.

"That sounds nice, and I like stories very much," the priest said. "They help me understand myself better."

The priest lit a cigarette and crossed his legs. Max stared at him.

"It's the only vice we're allowed," the priest said, exhaling. "Would you like one?"

Max raised a hand to say no.

"Did the story happen here in the Eternal City?" asked the priest.

"Las Vegas."

"Las Vegas?"

"Have you ever been to Las Vegas?" Max asked.

"No, I haven't, but I have seen it on a postcard."

"Imagine a woman sitting on a wall outside a casino."

"A woman?"

"Yes."

"Okay," the priest said, and closed his eyes. "I'm picturing it."

"A woman sitting on a wall outside a casino. It is very hot. The air smells of beer and perfume. The woman's name is Molly. She married quite young."

"A teenage bride?" the priest asked.

"Exactly—very young," Max said. "Molly's parents came from Fayette County but settled in Knox County—that's in Texas. Her father drove school buses, and her mother didn't work. Molly went to Knox County High. The school mascot was a bear. Some of the football players had tattoos of bear claws on their arms. There was a lake near the town. It was very popular with teenagers who liked to sit in trucks over-looking the water.

"From the postcard you've seen of Las Vegas, Father, imagine the ghostly band of neon which hangs above the city, changing the color of all the faces within its reach. The bright, flashing lights that promise children everything but deliver nothing.

"You can see Las Vegas from a distance: Look for the clump of risen metal on the horizon. If you approach at night, lights will beckon you from the black desert like a claw hand in a neon glove.

"Molly's first husband was run over and killed not long after the wedding. Then she met a high school football coach who was married.

"Molly and the coach met intimately once or twice a week for several years. When Molly found herself pregnant, the high school football coach pretended they'd never met.

"Molly's son didn't even cry when he was born in 1985. Molly thought he had an old soul. And for the first four years she raised him all by herself."

The priest smiled and lit another cigarette to show his commitment.

Max went on:

"So Molly was sitting on the wall outside the casino, and she was crying but so quietly that nobody could see—not even her four-year-old son who paced in small circles, following his own shadow. Every so often Molly reached out for him but did not touch any part of his body.

"The trip to Las Vegas was Jed's idea. Molly and Jed had been seeing each other seriously for three months. Jed managed a furniture warehouse. Jed insisted that Molly's boy call him 'Dad.' When the boy saw Jed's truck pull up in the yard, he would run into his mother's bedroom. Under her bed there was a pile of small plastic animals. But it wasn't the best place to wait until Jed left. To the little boy, it sounded like they were taking it in turns to die."

"We're just waiting for your father," Molly said. "He'll be here any minute."

She had been saying it for hours. There was nothing else to say. The first time she said it, her son replied:

"He's not my father."

"Well, he wants to be if you'll let him," his mother snapped.

The sounds of the casino spilled onto the sidewalk. The hollow metal rush of coins played through speakers. Drunk gamblers looked at their hands as ghost coins rushed between their fingers. Their lives would change if only they could hit the jackpot. Those who had loved them in the past would love them again. Every wrong could be righted. A man could straighten out his affairs if he had money—if he had beaten the odds. He could afford to be generous.

A waiter rushed past Molly and her son with a platter of delicious fruit. Then a thin couple in sunglasses holding hands. Then an old woman staggered into the road and was yelled at by a man on a motorcycle who swerved around her. Three men in suits carefully dragged a man with a ripped shirt onto the sidewalk. His feet trailed under him like two limp oars.

"Don't ever come back or you'll be arrested," one of the suited men said.

"Okay," the man said quietly, then picked up the coins that had fallen from his pocket. The little boy helped him. The man said, "Thanks, boy."

There was quiet for a while, and then the boy started to cry. He sat on the ground. He was wearing shorts and his legs were red from the sun. His socks had caterpillars on them. One had rolled into his shoe because they had walked so much.

By 3 AM, the boy and his mother were invisible to the gangs of drunk insurance salesmen, dentists from Orange County, gentlemen gamblers from small towns in Kentucky, and women going to or coming from their work in the casinos and topless bars.

The little boy's throat was so dry he licked the tears from his cheeks. At some point during the early morning, he took a sticker from his pocket and set it on the ground with the glossy cards of naked women that litter the sidewalks of Las Vegas.

A limousine stopped at a light. It was a wedding. The women inside were smoking and singing along to country music. The bride was young. She looked at Molly and screamed.

The boy removed his sandals and set them next to his mother's shoes, which had been shed long ago.

Molly's pocketbook with all her money was in Jed's truck.

"I'll keep control of the money," Jed had said.

The drive from Texas took four days. The boy kept throwing up because Jed smoked with the windows up and the air-conditioning on.

At night they all slept in the back on a mattress. The nights were cool. The sky glowed purple at dawn—then gold poured across the sky as the day was forged.

Molly's son was too afraid to ask his mother for the restroom. The thought of entering the casino made him feel nauseated. An hour or so later his underpants had mostly dried and the stinging upon the skin of his legs had given way to a slight tingling.

Then somebody approached him.

A man stood and watched the boy for some time; then he went away.

Then the man returned with something in his hand.

The boy felt a cold dish pushed against his bare thigh.

Then he noticed a figure standing over him.

"*Mangia*," the man said softly, and pointed to the white, creamy square of dessert in the dish.

The man was wearing black pants with a soft red sash for a belt. His shirt was heavy and long-sleeved, with black and white horizontal stripes.

"Tiramisu," the man said earnestly. "From the Venetian Hotel and Casino, a few streets from here—I just got it for you."

The boy squinted and turned to his mother. Molly eyed the stranger suspiciously through her swollen eyes.

"Don't worry, Mama," the stranger said to Molly. He pointed to himself with both hands. "*Amico*—friend."

Molly had pretty eyes. She had made many "friends" in her life that she would sooner forget.

"No thanks," she replied in a voice loud enough for passersby to overhear. Her voice was cracked with thirst and fatigue.

"Mommy—can I eat this?" her son said, and dipped his finger in the cream. "I think it's good."

Molly held the dish in her hand, inspected the contents, and then put the dish back on the wall. "Eat it and thank the man."

The man sat on the wall a few yards from them and lit a thin cigar. It smelled very sweet. He began to whistle. When the boy had finished the dessert, he slid over to the stranger and set the bowl down gently.

"I really like it," he said.

"We call it tiramisu. It means 'pick me up' in Italian."

Then the man leaned down to the boy's ear. His breath smelled of cigars.

"There's liquor in it too." He winked.

The boy peered down at the empty bowl. In its center were the colors of Las Vegas, held fast in a tiny pool of melted cream.

"Why do you speak like that?" the boy asked.

"My accent?" the man said.

The boy nodded despite never having heard the word "accent" before.

"I'm a gondolier—and the accent is from Italy."

"A gon . . ."

"Gondolier, *sì*."

"A goboleer?"

"*Sì*—do you know what that is?"

"Goddamn it!" his mother snapped without looking up. "Stop bothering the man."

"But Mom, he's nice."

"They're all nice at the beginning," she said.

The man winked at the boy and then stood up. He took three small oranges from his pocket.

"They were all nice at the beginning, Mama—but could they all juggle at the beginning?" the man said.

The little boy watched the balls rise and fall. He sensed the weight of each orange in his own small hands.

"The magic is in how you catch each ball at the last minute, before it's lost," the stranger explained.

"I want to try," the boy said.

The gondolier stopped juggling and reached down.

Max held the oranges in his hands and looked at them.

"They're too big for me."

"Ah!" the gondolier exclaimed, and from his pocket appeared three kumquats.

Molly laughed.

"Kumquats are the way to every woman's heart, my little friend."

The boy looked at his mother again. He wanted her to be happy. They were on vacation.

"We're waiting for my fiancé," Molly said. "He's just finishing up."

The little boy set the kumquats next to his shoes and said quietly to the gondolier:

"He's lost all our money, mister."

"He'll win it back," Molly said.

The gondolier sat with them and lit another cigar.

"Smoking is bad for you," the boy said.

The gondolier shrugged. "Did my grandmother tell you to say that?"

"No," the boy said. "I saw it on TV."

When Molly woke with a start, it was almost dawn. Her son was sleeping with his head against the gondolier's striped shirt. The gondolier smoked and stared at nothing. Molly wondered for a moment if it was the same cigar.

"You must think we're pathetic," she said.

The gondolier thought for a moment and then said:

"Would you permit me to perform one favor for you and your son?"

"I don't know," Molly said. "My fiancé may not be in a good mood when he comes out."

"Okay," the gondolier conceded. "It doesn't matter—I just thought you might like it."

Two small eyes between them bolted open.

"Might like what?" inquired a little voice.

"Might like to be honored guests on my gondola—through the canals of Venice."

The boy climbed up on his mother's lap.

"We have to do this," he said soberly.

Molly turned to the gondolier.

"I don't know why you're doing this for us—but if you were going to kill us, you probably would have done it by now."

Her son glared angrily at her.

"He's not going to kill us."

As they entered the Venetian Hotel and Casino, the gondolier raised his arms.

"Welcome to the most beautiful country in the world," he said.

The boy looked at the statues perched high up on the roof.

Their white marble skin glistened in the early morning sun, their hands forever raised, the fingers extended slightly with the poise of faith.

"I think they are holy saints, little one," the gondolier said. "They look out for me—and you too."

One of the statues was missing. There was a space on the roof where it had once stood.

"Where's that one?" the boy said.

"I don't know," the gondolier said thoughtfully. "But just think—*caro mio*, he could be anywhere."

"I think I believe in saints," the boy said, and considered how the missing saint might somehow be his real father.

"You truly believe in the saints, boy?"

"Yes. I do."

"Then you are an Italian, kid, through and through—a hot-blooded Italian. Can you do this?" The gondolier pressed his fingers together and shook them at the sky. The boy copied his movement. "Now say, 'Madonna.' "

The boy put his fingers together and shook them and said, "Madonna."

"Good, but louder, *caro*, louder!" the gondolier exclaimed.

"Madonna!" the boy screamed.

People looked at them.

"What does that mean?" Molly asked. "It's not a bad word, is it?"

"No, Mama, it means, simply: I am in love with this beautiful world."

The boy looked up at the saints, his fingers pushed together like a small church.

"Madonna!" he said in that delicate thin voice of all children.

The three of them strolled through the casino without talking.

A few lugubrious souls were perched at the slots. The machines roared with life.

Two black men in suits with arms crossed smiled at the gondolier.

"How you doing, Richard?" one of them said.

"Ciao," the gondolier replied in a low voice.

"Is your name Richard?" Molly asked.

"In another life."

"In Italy?" asked the boy.

"Another life, little one," the gondolier said.

"Actually, can you call me 'big one'?" the little boy asked.

The corridor was a long marble walkway with tall milky pillars. Then they reached a room with a thousand gold leaves painted on the wall. The boy looked up. Naked people in robes swam through color. There were scores of angels too—even baby ones with plump faces and rosy cheeks.

"Madonna!" the boy said.

As they neared the end of the room, they could hear music, a few notes from an instrument strapped to a man's belly.

"*Caro mio,*" the accordionist said when he saw the gondolier.

"*Ciao fratello*," the gondolier said. "Let me introduce you to my dear two friends from the old country."

Carlo smiled and moved his instrument from side to side. His fingers pressed buttons and the box emitted its unique croak. The rush of air into its belly was like breathing.

"It's nice," Molly said.

Carlo followed them at a distance of several yards, playing the same three notes over and over again. The little boy kept turning around to smile. He'd never felt so important. When they stopped walking, they were outside on a bridge.

The rising sun was visible through a crack between two towering casino buildings.

"See that, big one?" the gondolier said to the boy. "Every morning can be the beginning of your life—you have thousands of lives, but each is only a day long."

When the sun had passed above them and given itself to the world, a woman in a black dress brought out a tray. She was very tall, and her heels clicked along the stone bricks.

"Good morning," she said, and passed the tray of food to the gondolier.

Molly hesitated. "We didn't order this."

"No, no—it's from your friend," the woman said, then pointed to one of the many intricately arched balconies built into the façade of the casino. An unrecognizable figure from a great height began to wave. When the same three notes bellowed out into the square, the boy waved back.

On the tray were half a dozen Krispy Kreme glazed doughnuts and a small wine bottle with a rose in it.

"Venetian Donetti Rings," the gondolier marveled.

The boy stared at them. "They look nice," he said.

The gondolier sniffed one and handed it to his little friend. "They're fresh—only a few minutes old," he said.

"Like the day," the boy said. The gondolier nodded with enthusiasm.

There were also three very small cups, two filled with black coffee and a third with milk.

"Are these cups for children?" asked the boy.

"Yes," said the gondolier, "because no matter how big sons and daughters get, they will always be children in the eyes of their parents."

Molly laughed.

After breakfast, the gondolier took Molly and her son by the hand and led them to the edge of an enormous swimming pool that ran under bridges and skirted the edge of the main square.

There were strange boats floating, all tied together and bobbing in agreement.

"We should probably get back," Molly said.

"You're right, Mama," the gondolier said, "but one ride won't take long."

"*Jed* will have to wait for *us* now, Mom," the boy said.

"Shit," Molly said angrily.

"Why not?" the gondolier said.

"Come on, Max," Molly said.

Molly started walking away. Her son trailed reluctantly. He felt like crying again and his legs were stinging.

Molly abruptly turned back to the gondolier. "You don't know us."

The gondolier had not moved, as though he hoped she might turn back.

"Yes I do, Lola," the gondolier said without any trace of an Italian accent.

Molly stopped walking.

"Why did you call me that?"

The gondolier looked at his worn-out shoes.

"That was my daughter's name," he said with a shrug.

"Your daughter?"

"Yes—my beautiful daughter. That was her name."

Molly glared at him with anger and pity.

"Well, that's not my name."

"But it could be," the gondolier insisted. "It could have been."

"You're not even Italian, are you?"

"Mom," the boy said.

Molly stood looking but not looking at the gondolier. The boy tugged on her arm. Then the reality of what her life truly was flooded her.

She felt sick and tired.

Several birds blew across a clean sky—unaware of anything but their own tiny lives.

The boy let go of his mother's arm and squatted down.

His head fell limply into his hands. He took his sandals off. In the hot morning sun his legs had begun to sting again.

People walked around them.

Then Molly reached down and fixed his caterpillar sock.

"Put your shoes on if you want to go on the gondola," she said.

At the entrance to the boats there were other men dressed in the same striped shirts. They smoked and drank coffee in little cups. They raised their hands in greeting and nodded without smiling.

Within a few minutes, the gondolier, Molly, and her son were in the boat. The boy said the boat looked like a mustache. He held on to his mother's hand. He wanted her to know she had made the right decision. Hands have their own language.

The gondolier stood like a mechanical toy and pushed against the bottom of the blue water with a long pole. Everyone was watching. Carlo walked alongside them and played his three notes.

"*Buongiorno!*" the gondolier announced to passersby. A Japanese woman started clapping.

Molly marveled at the people on their balconies. The restaurants too were filling up. The sinister cast of characters who had passed them during the night had gone, and the city swelled with a softer, gentler group who rose with the sun and woke only at night to fetch glasses of water.

When they reached a wider stretch of the canal, the gondolier stepped down and opened the trunk upon which he had been standing. He undid the lock and lifted from it a large dark wooden box. He set it down on the bench between the trunk and the emerald seat upon which Molly and her son sat very close together.

"What is it?" asked the boy.

"You'll see, big one."

From the trunk, the gondolier took a thin but heavy black circle and placed it on top of the box. Then he turned a handle quickly and pulled over a thick metal arm with a needle at its end.

At first, Molly and the boy heard nothing but crackling. By the time the strong, sweet voice of Enrico Caruso echoed through the Venetian piazza, the gondolier was back on his trunk mouthing along to the words.

People flocked to the side of the bridge and applauded. Children stared in silent wonder.

The gondolier moved his mouth in perfect timing to the song. People thought he was really singing. But the voice was that of someone long dead.

Molly leaned back and closed her eyes. She had never heard a man sing with such emotion. She put her arm around her son and realized that the love she'd always dreamed of was sitting in the seat beside her wearing sandals and socks with caterpillars on them.

The song ended, but the needle kept going. The box crackled as they returned to where they had begun. The gondolier quickly tied his boat to the line of other boats. His hands were old and beaten like two worn-out dogs.

The gondolier sat down on the bench next to the music box.

"Again," the boy said.

The gondolier wound up the machine as he had done before. At the sound of crackling, the other gondoliers stopped what they were doing and turned to face him. He stood proudly on his trunk, cleared his throat, and began to sing.

The piercing beauty of a lone voice soared determinedly from the canal into the piazza, drawing people from beds and flat-screen televisions to the edges of their balconies.

For a few moments, the voice was even audible in the casino; cards were set down; heads tilted upward.

"What's the song about?" the boy whispered to his mother.

"I don't know," Molly said.

"I do," her son said.

The piazza crackled with applause.

When it came time to say good-bye, the little boy didn't want to let go of the gondolier. They could feel the beating of each other's hearts.

In the Square of St. Peter, the lines outside the tomb had grown very long. Young Italian men in jeans sold water and apples. Tour guides stood still and held paddles. Children fell asleep in carriages. Teenagers tore past on smoking scooters. Restaurant managers heckled passing tourists, who stopped for a moment and then kept walking.

Occasionally, someone looked up and noticed that a statue was missing.

The priest took a handkerchief from his pocket and dabbed his eyes.

"Madonna," he said quietly.

And before parting, the two men thought of a lone gondolier paddling the canals of a swimming pool in the Nevada desert—reeling in the forsaken with the song he had once sung to his daughter on a farm in Wisconsin.

The Coming and Going

of Strangers

Walter's Journey Through the Rain

WALTER WHEELED HIS HOT, ticking motorbike up and down the muddy lane, breathing with the rhythm of a small, determined engine. Fists of breath hovered and then opened over each taken-step. He would soon be within sight of his beloved's house. In the far distance, Sunday parked over the village like an old mute who hid his face in the hanging thick of clouds. The afternoon had seen heavy rain and the fields were soft.

Tired and wet, lovesick Walter thought of the Sunday town streets, hymns and hot dinners, the starch and hiss of ironing; shoes polished and set down before the fire so that each shoe held a flame in its black belly; dogs barking at back doors. Early stars.

He stopped and held his motorbike still. He listened for the sounds of the faraway town. At first he could hear only his own hard breathing. Then a bus growling up the hill; the creaking of trees; and then in the distance—seagulls screaming from the cliffs.

There were scabs of mud on the black fuel tank of Walter's motorbike. Leaves and sticks had caught in the spokes and marked the stages of his journey in their own language. Light had not yet drained from the world, yet the moon was already out and cast a skeletal spell upon the bare branches of trees.

The road sloped downward for several hundred yards. In the distance, cows perched on steep pasture and barked solemnly out to sea. Walter imagined their black eyes full of wordless questions. What were they capable of understanding? The cold country of water that lay beyond the cliffs? Did they feel the stillness of a Sunday?

Walter removed the basket of eggs from the milk crate strapped to the back of his seat. Then he lay the machine down on its side. A handlebar end disappeared into a puddle.

It was the highest point in the county. Looking west, Walter knew from the few books in his uncle's caravan that America lay beyond. He exhaled and imagined how night—like a rolling wave—would carry his breath across the sea to New York. He imagined a complete stranger breathing the air that filled his own body.

Walter removed a glove and rubbed his face. The dirt beneath his fingernails was black with oil. Walter pictured his mother back at home, sitting by the fire with Walter's baby brother in her arms—wondering what her son was doing out in the drizzle. His father would be out of his wheelchair and up on the roof of the caravan, whistling and hammering new panels above the sink where the leak was.

"This country is nothing but rain and songs," his father once said in his Romany accent.

A young Walter had asked if that was good.

"Ay, it's grand, Walter—because every song is a shadow to the memory it follows around, and rain touches a city all at once with its thousand small hands."

Walter loved The Smiths. In the caravan last week, as his mother sat him down for a haircut, Walter showed her a picture of Morrissey.

"Who in the world is that skinny fella?" she'd said.

"Can you cut my hair like that—can you do it, Ma?"

"Why would you want it all on one side?"

Walter shrugged. "It's what I want," he said.

"All right—if that's what you want."

"Thanks, Ma."

"He's a pop singer, is he?"

Walter sighed. "He's a little bit more than that, Ma." Then Walter thought, How could any sane woman turn me down if I looked like one of The Smiths—which in his Romany Irish accent sounded like "The Smits."

One night, long ago, Walter's father sang his own song to seduce a woman he'd just met. She listened with her hands in the sink. She fell in love holding a dinner plate. It was not how she'd pictured it.

Then several years later, he metered softly a different song to baby Walter as rain beat down upon the roof of the wind-rocked caravan.

The Gypsies on the Hill

WALTER'S FAMILY HAD LIVED outside the village of Wicklow on the east coast of Ireland for Walter's whole life. Unlike the rest of his Romany family, Walter's had stayed in one place, and contrary to Rom custom, Walter was encouraged to attend the local school and mingle with the people of the village.

Everyone in the village knew who Walter was, and they knew why his family lived on the hill a mile or so outside town.

In 1943, Walter's two sets of grandparents escaped Hitler's murderous dream and came to Ireland. In the early 1960s, at a Rom festival in the south of Ireland, Walter's mother and father met in a sloping field. It was quite dark, but they could see each other's faces. The evening was chilly. She was barefoot. Walter's father asked one of her brothers where they were from. Then later on, he offered her some cake to eat. She took it from his hands and put it straight into her mouth without chewing. They both laughed. Later on she hears a knock on the caravan door. Her brother is reading. She is barefoot at the sink with her sleeves rolled up. Her brother knows who it is. He opens the door and goes out to smoke. The man is holding a guitar. Finally it's happening, and she holds her breath.

Two nights later, they ran away. Then, as was the custom, their families met and laughed and argued in equal amounts. Within a week, bride price was set and Walter's parents (then in their teens) returned home.

Walter's young mother and father journeyed to Wicklow immediately after the ceremony, even though everyone joked about how they'd already taken their honeymoon.

"It's such a fine, wild, and desolate country," Walter's father said to his bride in the car on the drive. He was still quite nervous because she was a quiet girl. He spread a blanket across her knees. She shivered—though it wasn't cold.

Her camp was near Belfast, while his camp was always moving, mostly around Dublin.

Both families made a living from selling used cars, car parts, and scrap metal, sharpening knives, and laying tarmac. The women told fortunes—a craft developed and perfected over centuries and based on the idea that all humans want the same thing: love and acceptance.

After passing through the village, the young couple parked on a hill and began to pitch a marital tent in a field overlooking the sea. The tent was orange, and its sides were hung over cool hollow poles that fit inside one another.

Once it was up, they lay inside under a thick blanket and told stories without trying. Outside the tent, clouds blew across the field and out to sea.

A rabbit hopped up to the tent, then ran back into the hedgerow.

After they were together, her body trembled. She pressed herself against him. He listened to the sounds of night and of the sea wrapping its cold arms around the thick rocks; the white froth of saltwater; a chorus of popping barnacles.

In the morning, Walter's father cooked a breakfast with food they'd brought—food that wasn't polluted by non-Romany shadows.

As half a dozen sausages thopped and spat, turning brown on one side, Walter's mother heard a tiny splash. She was washing her face beside the hedge. The water was mouse gray. She turned and looked back at the tent; its tangerine orange sides billowed in the wind against the hard green of the hedgerow. She continued washing. It was such a windy day.

Then Walter's father heard something— a feeble scream in the distance. He looked up from his sausages and saw two specks on the cliff several hundred yards away. He dropped his fork in the grass and ran. Two children stood at the edge beside an empty stroller. The older child was heaving violently and looking down at the water.

Then the young child started to scream.

At least a hundred feet down in the sea, something bobbed.

The water was dark green.

Walter's father kicked off his boots and then jumped.

When he hit the water, several bones in his right foot split.

His wife saw him disappear. She opened her mouth to scream, but no sound emerged.

Everyone thought they were dead because there was simply no trace of either of them. The police launched a boat. Not even a sock or a small shoe. Not a trace.

Walter's mother was taken to the children's house by the police and given tea, which normally she wouldn't have been able to drink because of Romany custom.

The mother of the children sat very close to Walter's mother. Eventually they held hands.

The children sat at their feet.

They were still and their faces were empty.

More family trickled in through the thick farm door. People screamed and then talked quietly. An unmarried uncle sobbed into his hand. Then two women of the family approached the Gypsy in the chair. They touched her shoulders, knees, and then held on tight because it was too late—too late for anything except blind, gentle, wordless touching.

Then the sound of breaking glass upstairs.

Men's voices.

The sound of something heavy hitting the floor.

Time unraveling without notice.

Then suddenly—a miracle.

Almost midnight and the police are pounding on the door.

Lights go on.

People in chairs come to life.

The fire is a dark blood orange.

More screaming, but a different kind as a man and small girl are helped from the back of a police car.

The man is dark-skinned. A Romany. The child clings to him.

They are wrapped in thick blankets. They both have messy hair. The child is too afraid to take her eyes off the Gypsy who jumped off a cliff to save her. His face has never been so still. He's not fully convinced they're alive. Not until he sees his wife will he believe it's not a dream—a fantasy prelude to the life beyond death.

The mother loses a shoe as she runs for the frightened bundle of child. The child reaches out, then once buried in the familiar bosom explodes with tears and shrieks.

Walter's mother slaps her husband across the face, then kisses it all over.

More headlights turn into the driveway.

The rattle of teacups from the kitchen.

Joy fills the house.

Men grab the hair on one another's heads.

Screaming and jumping.

The sound of breaking glass.

Singing.

The Gypsy and the girl were found together walking up the cliff road toward town. They had been swept several miles from the spot where the child had fallen in. The outgoing tide had pulled them away from the rocks.

His arms were raw, burning.

His black eyes blazed with the fury of staying alive.

Soaked clothes weighing them down.

Finally man and child dumped upon a shallow sandbar, then carried up the beach on the spreading foam of a breaker.

Walter's father had lost all sense of time. Perhaps years had passed. Perhaps they were the only two people alive on earth. Perhaps they would live together from now on. Such thoughts entered his mind as he watched the child cough and cough and cough.

Walter's father removed all her clothes and tucked her frigid body under his clothes so that only her head stuck out. As her body sucked the heat from his, she quieted and fell asleep.

She was not dead, he knew that. He could feel her breathing. He could feel her life attached to his.

Finally a car in the distance. Walter's father signaled weakly.

"Fuck off, Gypo," the driver shouted through his window.

More walking.

Then an old farmer with a wagonful of sheep.

He had been in the war and recognized immediately that desolate look of the figure in his headlights.

The farmer saw that the man walking up the dark road was soaked through. Then he noticed a second head. He pulled to the side of the road and hurried them into his wagon, freeing several sheep to make room. Then he drove back to his house without stopping to close the gate.

His wife found blankets. Sugar lumps dropped liberally into china cups.

The farmer watched the fire and wondered if they might stay.

It wasn't until Walter had stopped shivering that he told the farmer how the little girl wasn't his—that he'd simply found her beneath the surface in the swirling black, in the cold, their arms like vines destined to forever entangle.

The farmer looked very serious.

His wife telephoned the police from the hall phone.

The next day, as Walter's father and mother were packing up their orange tent, several old Land Rovers turned in to the field through an open gate. Then several more cars. Even a police car. Walter's mother helped her husband stand. His leg was bandaged. The pain was like fifty wasps trapped inside his foot.

A large group of people walked toward them, headed by the children from the cliff and their parents. They stopped walking several yards off and the little girl's father approached Walter's father. He stood opposite and extended his hand. When Walter's father went to shake it, the young man simply leaned forward and hugged him. Several people in the group started clapping. The policeman removed his hat. Women made the sign of the cross upon their anoraks.

The man handed Walter's father an envelope.

"For what you done, Gypsy," the man growled. His cheeks glistened.

Walter's father looked at the envelope.

"It's a letter from me to you, and a deed. We're giving you this here land we stand on."

Walter's father had been warned about getting mixed up in the affairs of non-Romanies.

"Take it," the man insisted. "Mary, Mother of Jesus, take it, man."

Walter looked up at the sky and exhaled.

What would his family say if he started deal-making with non-Romanies.

Then the father broke down. Two men stepped forward and propped him up.

Then the sister of the saved child ran over to Walter's father and took his dark hand.

"We don't care that you're Gypsies," she said.

Walter's mother stood by her husband.

"You can bring your whole family here if you like," the girl continued. "We can all be together—it'll be like heaven."

And so the orange tent was never taken down. Instead, the camp was built around it, and they became known as the "Gypsies on the Hill."

And when the father of the saved girl decided to move his family to the safety of Dublin a year later, he made a sign in his metal shop and erected it on the cliff one windy afternoon.

It read:

> *On this spot in 1963,*
> *An Irish Gypsy jumped off the cliff*
> *To save my daughter.*

About the time the sign went up, Walter was conceived.

The Canadian Orphan

WALTER LOOKED AT HIS motorcycle on its side in
the puddle. He imagined firing up the engine and
riding at full pelt toward her house. In the distance waves
crashed against the point: the foam, the black rocks—two
equally determined forces. Walter felt such forces alive
within himself. He thought of his father's daring rescue before he was born.

Walter was headed for the very same farmhouse his
mother had been taken to after her husband tossed his body
off the cliff into the sea.

After the saved child's family moved to Dublin, a middle-
aged man moved in and began to farm the area around his
cottage. Now, strangely, it was the home of Walter's beloved.
The orphan from Canada.

Walter lifted his bike off its side and continued toward
her house. Only a mile or so to go.

He wondered if he might even find out her name—that
would be a brilliant start, he thought. He imagined riding
his bike off a cliff and screaming her name in midair.

Walter was riding his motorbike the first time he saw her
in the village. He veered off the road and almost hit an old
woman.

"Dear God in heaven," he muttered to himself as his eyes
followed her from shop to shop. "What a beauty, mother of

Jesus." The old woman glared at him and waved her stick.

Walter assumed the girl was an American tourist, one of the many who would appear (usually in late summer) with their children and announce themselves in the pub as descendants of so-and-so.

Walter watched her stroll through the village quietly, lingering at shop windows. Then he smoked and pretended not to watch her wait for the N36 bus, which deposited its passengers about the northern part of the countryside every time it pulled to the side of the road.

Walter considered following the bus into the country, but his bike was so noisy it might irritate her, and there was the fear that the bus might end up going faster than he could.

Walter resolved to discover who she was and where she lived from the people in the shops, who between them knew everything that was happening within a twenty-mile radius.

At the newsagent, Walter asked for a pack of twenty Players cigarettes and casually mentioned that he'd seen a stranger in the village—a girl walking alone like a single cloud in the sky—but then his breath shallowed suddenly and he was unable to continue talking.

"You should really think about cutting down," the news-agent said, holding up the cigarettes. "You're only a lad to be smoking so much; look at you, Walter—you can barely breathe."

Before Walter left the shop, the newsagent suddenly remembered what Walter had said and called out.

"Ay, the girl you're talking about, Walter. She's been in, nice girl she is, and very tall, and a bit too old for you, me boy, if you know what I mean—a little too experienced." Then he laughed to himself. Walter shrugged and felt his blood turn cold with embarrassment.

"I'm actually getting on in years," Walter exclaimed.

Just as he was about to step outside, he heard the newsagent add, "And very sad what happened to her and her sister."

Walter poked his head back around the door.

"What's that you say?"

"Very sad, Walter—what happened to her ma and dad."

Walter stepped inside the shop again. It was brighter this time. He reached for a pint of milk and took it up to the counter.

"I bet you didn't know she's Canadian."

"Canadian? That's nice," Walter said, pretending not to care.

"And she arrived in Ireland with her sister sometime last month. Popsy met them at the airport—"

"How does Popsy know them?" Walter asked.

"I heard it was the first time Popsy had been to an airport, and he asked the Aer Lingus girl where exactly on the runway did the people come out."

The newsagent cackled.

"What a daft bugger he is, eh?" the newsagent said.

Walter rolled his eyes.

"So what happened to her family?" Walter said, taking his change and tucking the milk into his jacket.

"Well, me boy—they all perished in a fiery car crash outside Toronto."

"In Canada?"

"Ay. Now all that's left of the family is the tall girl that you saw, her young sister—who's the spitting image of her—and daft old Popsy."

The newsagent sniggered.

"That man's lived alone his entire life—and now he's got two girls to take care of. Jesus, Mary, and Joseph—what next?"

"Ay, it's strange, it is," Walter said.

"But something tells me he'll do all right," the news-agent admitted in a gesture that was particularly Irish—to cajole, mock, embarrass as a prelude to love.

"How's your da?"

"He's fine," Walter said.

"Still in the wheelchair?"

"Ay—but it's grand how he gets around."

"Ay—they don't make 'em like your da anymore. Give him my regards."

"Ay, I will," Walter promised.

Walter slipped from the bright shop and stepped out into the dusk. His motorcycle headlamp was on and cast a web of yellow light across the black concrete.

Walter had never talked directly with Popsy but knew who he was. The man had never married. He lived alone in an isolated farmhouse on the cliffs. He was occasionally seen in the pub—generally in the summer—talking amiably in his soft voice and telling his dog to lie down. Walter didn't know his real name but knew he was a master carpenter. Walter's father had once said that what Popsy did with wood made it stronger than steel.

Walter continued in the rain along the wet farm road with his basket of eggs in the back. A bird dipped alongside him and glided forward, landing on the road ahead to gulp down a worm.

When Walter was seven, he learned to swim on the incoming tide, watched vigilantly by his uncle, who'd come to live at their camp when Walter was a baby. His uncle had wanted to marry a non-Romany girl from Sethlow, but she eventually left him for an Englishman who worked on an oil rig. However, Uncle Ivan didn't seem particularly upset when the girl one day turned up with her new boyfriend at the camp in a brown Rover. In fact, Uncle Ivan had laughed and shaken the new boyfriend's hand vigorously.

Walter (now that he was older) believed the real reason that Uncle Ivan came to live with them was because of Walter's father's accident, which left him partially paralyzed. Walter's father could feel his legs and stand on them (with great pain), but he was unable to walk—or to work. Uncle Ivan had the sort of energy that enabled him to do two men's work in half the time. And he was also a celebrity. Uncle Ivan was the only Gypsy (and Irishman) in history to win a gold medal at the Olympics.

The Trampolining Gypsy

U NCLE IVAN HAD ONCE lived in the caravan that now
belonged to Walter. Upon the walls, newspaper clip-
pings the color of salt and pepper displayed the impossible:
a white figure flying through the air.

As a child, Walter liked to stand very still in front of
each clip and study the expressions on his uncle's face. In
the grainy prints, Uncle Ivan always wore a white under-
shirt with a number on it, white shorts tied at the front,
thin black socks, and black Brogues.

Walter remembered his own bony white body stretching
out in the cold water as he learned to swim. His uncle would
call out strokes from the beach. Sometimes waxy slabs of sea-
weed hung in the water. Walter didn't like it. He imagined
other things lurking at the bottom. One autumn day while
swimming, Walter was bitten on the thigh by a conger eel.
At first it felt like something was scratching him—maybe
a dumb jellyfish washed in from deep water—then Walter
looked down and saw a black head and an impossibly thick
body writhing about his legs. Walter remembers his uncle's
shirt tied around the wound. Watery blood running down
his thigh, dripping off his big toe.

His uncle carried him a mile up the hill at a jog, and
then the local doctor came. The doctor was from the north
of Ireland and drove a Mercedes Estate. He looked at every-

one from under his glasses. He balanced a mint imperial on his tongue during the examination. Several days in bed with the black-and-white television brought in from the living room, and anything he wants to eat, was the doctor's advice.

His uncle sat faithfully at his bedside the whole time, smoking, feeding him sausages, and telling him what a man he was, to have been bitten by a conger and survive— it was unthinkable. Walter still had the scar; a white line, jagged but no longer raised.

Then Uncle Ivan would fry up a dozen pieces of black pudding and they'd eat in front of the television.

His uncle had loved cold weather and kept fit by running in singlet and shorts on mornings too cold even for school.

Broken Eggs

THEN THE RAIN STOPPED.

The landscape stretched before Walter like in a painting—lines of dark green hedgerows, a cluster of bare trees, an ancient gate hung during harvest, dots of hill-sheep and then the fabric of sea.

The morning Walter found Uncle Ivan stiff in his bed, snow had blown in through an open window and covered his body. In his will, Uncle Ivan had left his caravan, the motorbike, and his Olympic gold medal to Walter.

Walter watched the thread of smoke rise up from his beloved's farmhouse in the distance. The medal lay flat upon his chest, inside his shirt. He could feel the weight of it pulling on the back of his neck like an omen of hope and success.

The cake at Uncle Ivan's funeral was in the shape of a trampoline. The baker had made a frame of drinking straws over the cake from which dangled a marzipan figure.

At the burial, someone read a newspaper story written about the deceased in 1972. The story was called "In Mid-Flight an Irish Gypsy Soars."

Walter was almost at the farmhouse. He repeated the headline over and over to himself, with the voice the priest used when he read from the Old Testament in assembly.

"In mid-flight an Irish Gypsy soars."

"In mid-flight an Irish Gypsy soars."

Then Walter thought of his own headline.

"In love with a Canadian girl, a Romany hero soars."

Walter's leather jacket and trousers were heavy with water. He could feel the last few drops of rain bouncing off his helmet. He'd ridden twenty miles through plump green valleys. Sheep raised their curly heads to see him speed noisily by. The long lane down to the cold farmhouse was full of deep puddles, the moon in each puddle like a small white anchor, and the pale honey of windows in the distance.

Walter imagined her walking around the house, like a beautiful thought wandering around someone's head.

Walter pushed his bike through the gate. He could sense her breathing beneath his, and he felt her hands reach out from the handlebars and curl around his black gloves. He imagined how she would throw aside the basket of eggs and by the time they smashed against the stone floor, she would be kissing him wetly on the lips. In the dark, he might look even more like Morrissey.

By wheeling his motorbike instead of riding it, Walter might have a chance to sit and watch her through the window before knocking on the door and asking her uncle Popsy, quite innocently, if he might want some of the eggs left over from the morning's collection.

Walter had spent the early part of the day picking out the best eggs from the chicken hatch and reciting William

Blake's *Songs of Innocence* to the hens, which stared at him angrily, then clucked away in panic.

After laying each egg out by his caravan, Walter found an old toothbrush and filled a bucket with warm soapy water.

As Walter scrubbed the feathers and burnt yellow feces from the shell of each egg, he noticed that his mother, father, and baby brother were watching him through the low window of their caravan. Walter's father was sitting in his wheelchair with the baby on his lap. His mother was standing up in her fluffy slippers. She knocked on the thin pane of glass with her knuckle.

"Walter, you cleaning the eggs now, is it?"

"Do you want a cup of tea?" his father shouted from his wheelchair. After reaching for something too heavy, he'd fallen the wrong way. He lay there for several hours wondering what his life would be like.

Birds filled the sky before anyone came. Then a coworker discovered him.

A doctor in Limerick believed that within ten years, they'd have the technology to fix him. He wasn't paralyzed, they said—it was something to do with nerves. Everyone said it was the fall from the cliff—that his back had never been the same.

Walter liked to push his father along the road. The thin black tires glistened after rolling through thin puddles.

Cars would slow down at the sight of them, and each face would stare blankly out.

The last time Walter had pushed his father to the new supermarket a couple of miles from the caravan, Walter noticed how the hair on his father's head was very soft. On the way back from the supermarket after a lunch of doughnuts and strong, sweet tea, his father's thinning crown made Walter want to cry; the vague idea that the seated figure before him—the king of dads, hunched in his chair—was not Walter's father but his son or his brother; and that life was a lottery of souls.

Walter took his business with the eggs into his small caravan and continued his work earnestly. When each egg was so shiny that it balanced a smaller version of the caravan window upon its shell, Walter sat on his Honda 450, which he kept inside next to his bed (a very un-Romany thing to do), and smoked one of his Players cigarettes. He liked the way his motorcycle looked under the single hanging bulb.

The corners of the ceiling were softened by thick cobwebs. The caravan had once been Uncle Ivan's. It now belonged to Walter, and Walter loved it, as he would love no other house for the rest of his life, no matter how grand or expensive or unique.

Walter was nine when Uncle Ivan decided he wanted electric lights.

Walter's eggs sat in a line upon the table, touching one another so as not to roll away. The table had once supported the weight of his uncle's elbows as he studied the lightbulb on that long-ago afternoon.

After hours of wiring and cursing, Uncle Ivan slowly screwed the bulb into its neat socket. Walter's mother and father were summoned from their caravan. Ivan had wanted Walter to push the switch that would bring it to life, but in the end he was not allowed. Uncle Ivan was an Olympian, not an electrician, Walter's mother had said.

They all cheered as the bulb suddenly glowed with the push of a button.

"What a miracle," said his uncle. "It's like there's a slither of sun in there."

"It's about time you got the electric in your van, Ivan," Walter's mother had said.

The four of them sat under it for some time without a word until his mother finally said:

"Look at us sitting here like idiots."

Uncle Ivan stood up and turned the switch on and off several times before they all went down to the pub for an early drink from glasses the barmaid was happy to keep away from the other glasses. You must understand that the Romany rituals of cleanliness are symbolic, not practical.

Walter wondered why he had thought of the lightbulb. And then he realized that his heart was also small and bright and hot. He would deliver the eggs that very afternoon, lest the bulb mysteriously flicker and die.

Walter turned around and saw his mother standing in the doorway.

"So who are the eggs for?"

"Nobody," Walter said.

"A girl, is it?"

Walter nodded.

His mother kissed him on the cheek.

"Your dear father was the same way for me," she said. "But he never polished me an egg a day in his life."

She handed Walter a cup of tea.

"Just don't start that thing up unless you've strapped your helmet on. I don't know why you keep it in here—your Romany ancestors would turn in their graves."

As she shuffled back past her small garden in her slippers, she stopped to unpeg several socks hanging on the line. Walter saw his oily handprints on the back of her blouse.

A few moments later, Walter heard laughing from their caravan.

Then Walter imagined his mother lying down with her husband and closing her eyes, the baby in a soft sleep in the back bed. Everything warm and dark. Raining again outside. The tapping of it against the window.

Then later, the baby quietly awake in his crib, playing with his feet and watching clouds move like gentle friends.

Walter leaned his bike against a tree and crept up to the kitchen window. He slowly lifted his head to see inside.

"Oh, my love, my love," he gasped, and his gaze like a net reached over her.

Walter pressed himself against the cold stones of the house as close to the glass pane as he dared. In her outstretched hand was a half-eaten apple. The white flesh glistened. She chewed slowly, occasionally touching her hair.

Walter longed for something to happen—a fire, a flood, some biblical catastrophe that would afford him an opportunity to rush in and rescue her.

Her uncle tended the fire dispassionately, and then sat down again. They were watching a black-and-white television and not talking. With their eyes safely fixed upon the screen, Walter wiped the window with his sleeve, but the mist was on the inside.

His body went limp as he let his eyes explore the length of her body. Her legs were so long, they stretched out almost the length of the table. Her young sister was nowhere to be seen—perhaps in her bedroom playing with dolls, Walter mused. Walter imagined her talking to them, smoothing out their clothes with her small fingers and setting them down at a table of plastic plates and plastic food which she held to their lips encouragingly.

Then a gentle but powerful feeling took Walter, and the boy immediately understood the obsession of the portrait artists he'd read about in his uncle's books; the troubadour poets and their sad buckled horses; the despairing souls who rowed silently at dusk in a heavy sea; the wanderers, the lost, those dying blooms who'd fallen away.

Walter's young mind reeled at the power of his first feeling of love. He would have walked to America if she had promised to meet him there.

From where had these feelings come? Walter thought. For he had not swallowed anything created by her body; neither had there been any physical contact, not even the brushing of sleeves in a crowded market. So these feelings for her—like fires lit in various parts of his body—must always have been within him, waiting to be lit.

And then Walter thought of something else. Could it be that first love was the only true love? And that after those first fires had been doused or burned out, men and women chose whom they would love based on worldly needs, and then reenacted the rituals and feelings of that first pure experience—nursed the flames that once burned of their own accord. . . .

Walter declared in his thoughts that his virginity was spiritual and that he had already lost it to someone he was yet to meet. The physical act, should it ever occur, would be nothing more than blind and fumbling reassurance that man's mortality could be celebrated with the division of spirit through flesh.

Walter wondered what else he was capable of—what other emotions, talents, even crimes might suddenly erupt under certain conditions.

He remembered all those mornings as a child out in the field beside his caravan, watching storms move across the fields below. Eyes glued to the sky until a fork of lightning hit the earth; wind ripping trees from soggy riverbanks; an early morning blizzard like pillows ripped open. Walter suddenly felt that such things were part of his very being. And that for his entire life, the countryside he'd grown up in was a form of self-portrait.

And with his mind churning experience to understanding like milk into butter, Walter thought of Adam and Eve, the inevitable fall—their mouths stuffed with apple; their lips dripping with the sweet juice of it; the knowledge that life was the fleeting beauty of opposites, that human existence was the result of conflict, of physical and spiritual forces trapped within a dying vessel.

Every change in his behavior started making sense to him.

The days after seeing her, Walter took long rides on the roads he imagined she might be out walking. He dreamed of stopping to offer her a lift.

Walter would ride for miles and miles, as far as he could on a full tank—through the wind and pelting rain which lashed his face. Then he'd find a petrol station in the twilight and fill his tank while being watched suspiciously by the cashier from the bright kiosk that sold crisps, chocolate, Pot Noodle, magazines (dirty ones on the top shelf), birthday cards, cigarettes, maps, and black pudding.

The greatest hazard to riding a small motorcycle through the countryside of Ireland was the wildlife—sheep in particular, who when they spotted Walter rattling along would hurl themselves into the road.

The evening matured into night. Walter shivered. It had stopped raining, but his clothes were wet through. Standing at the window, he began to feel cold.

When she laughed at something on the television, Walter laughed too. There was a moment when she turned and peered through the glass, failing to notice the face of a boy upon the pane like an unfinished painting.

What he'd read in books was not right—man did not love with his heart but with his whole body. Every piece of him was involved somehow—he could feel her in his legs, in his fingers, the imagined weight of her shoulders upon his, her head upon his bare white chest. Walter knew he would die for her. And he thought of all the old songs he'd heard, the ancient ones from the days of horses, candles, and hunks of meats spitting on open fires. The songs composed for men at sea, the sweet high voices of girls imploring the Lord to bring home their loves. Walter imagined himself one of these men, called from the frosty woods to her cottage by singing, his horse nodding through the marsh, hands blistered from wet reins, breath in the cold like white fire.

Walter knelt and coughed into the patch of wet grass at his feet. Then he sat down knowing that on the other side of the wall was his eternal love. He could sense the weight of her body in the chair. He wanted to touch himself in the way Father McCarthy had forbidden all young boys to do in assembly—and he would have but for the sense that in some way it would have defiled his pure love for her.

His fingers dug into the soil as he imagined the vibration of her voice touch his body. He stiffened. His mouth hung open. And then he sprang back at the shock of seeing a figure standing a few yards from him.

"Mary, Mother of Jesus!"

"What are you doing out here?" a small, trembling voice said. It was a little girl. The younger sister, wearing an overcoat and orange Wellington boots that were too big for her. A plastic hairless doll hung down from one of her hands.

"Don't you have a television at home?" she said.

"What? A television?"

"Is that your motorcycle by the tree?"

"My what?"

She turned and pointed.

"Oh, my motorcycle—yes, it's mine."

"Can you take us for a ride?" she asked.

"Us?" Walter said, suddenly hopeful. "Us?"

The girl held up her doll.

"Ay," Walter said. "I'll take you and your dolly for a ride."

The girl's eyes widened with excitement. She said something in her doll's ear.

"But you have to tell me something first," Walter said quietly.

"Okay."

"Does your sister have a boyfriend in Canada?"

The girl looked back at his motorcycle.

"Are those eggs for us?"

"They might be—but first you have to tell me if your sister has a boyfriend."

"A boyfriend?"

"Some awful, boring fellow who tried to impress your sister but who just ended up being a nuisance without even realizing she was beyond him in every way imaginable. Did you notice anyone like that at all?"

"I don't think so," she said, unsure as to whether it was the right answer. Then in a voice loud enough to be heard from inside, she said, "Are you in love with my sister—is that why you've brought us a basket of eggs?"

Walter felt the tingling of embarrassment.

"It's more complicated than that, you know——you're too young to understand."

"Are you going to marry her?"

"Is that a serious question?" Walter said.

The girl nodded.

"Do you think she'd like me?"

She nodded enthusiastically. "I think she would."

"Well, that's a brilliant start," Walter said with pure joy. "I'm Walter, by the way."

"I'm Jane," the girl said, with the embarrassment of all children when talking to someone older.

Walter didn't care that he was speaking to a girl of eight or nine. Through the cold autumn night, he could hear the bells of the church casting their notes upon the village like seeds. He could see Father McCarthy's serious face as they approached the altar. The Canadian orphan in white like the queen of swans, her eyes like tiny glaciers that held him, the church, the congregation, the whispering smoke of incense; old women's heads in colored hats, bowing like yesterday's flowers. He would wear his motorcycle jacket and Uncle Ivan's Olympic medal.

"What should I do, Jane?"

"It's a bit cold out here," Jane said.

"Well, go on in," Walter said. "You'll catch your death."

Then he regretted saying it as he remembered what had happened to her parents only several months ago.

"I'm sorry about your ma and dad."

Jane set down her doll.

"Don't worry, Jane—they're up in heaven, and when you've had a long life and your own babies you can see them again, so don't worry now, they're not really dead, they're just not here."

Jane went back into the house with her doll.

Walter listened for the sound of the latch and considered for a moment that she might tell the uncle, and then he'd be discovered and would have to explain what he was doing.

He imagined her uncle coming out in black boots. His kind face quickly turning to scorn. Jane pointing at the hot, wet ball of boy in the thicket beneath the window. Then his beloved—ashamed and disgusted, surveying him from afar; a shawl over her shoulders like closed black wings.

What would he say? By the next Sunday, the entire village would think him a Peeping Tom.

But you can't explain love, Walter thought to himself, and with the breathless ambition of youth, he believed, in his young heart, that those five words would be enough to shield him.

"You can't explain love," he said out loud. "That's how it gets ruined."

Without daring to look in again, Walter decided he had to go—but that he would allow himself to return. He would leave the eggs at the door with one of his gloves—then he'd have to return to pick it up. He'd started to rise when he heard the latch of the front door.

His heart rolled like a stone ball into his stomach.

"It's just me," Jane whispered. She handed Walter a lukewarm mug of tea.

"Jesus of Nazareth," Walter said, gulping back the tea in gulps. "You're a little star, Jane—but you bloody well gave me fright."

Inside the house, Uncle Popsy searched in vain for the tea he thought he'd set on the hall table only moments ago.

When the mug was empty, Jane pointed past the cottage and into the night.

"We have to go down to the sea now," she said, and Walter noticed that in one of her small hands were two red buckets, the kind children used to build sand castles.

"The sea? Why, Jane?" Walter asked.

"Because," she said, "I'm not allowed to go by myself."

"But you don't know me."

"Yes I do," she said emphatically.

Walter sighed. "You want to go there now?"

Jane nodded.

"In the dark?" Walter said.

Jane nodded. "It has to be now," she said, and pointed up at the moon.

"What about your uncle?"

"He's watching TV with my sister," Jane said. "Can we go on your motorcycle?"

"No."

"Please?"

"Absolutely not."

Jane stood and looked at him. She lifted her doll up to Walter's face, so they were at eye level.

"Please," the doll said without moving its mouth. "Don't be boring."

"Jesus, Jane—it's too feckin' loud."

Jane looked at her feet. Her bottom lip protruded slightly from the rest of her mouth.

"All right, " Walter said. "But if we go, we go on foot."

Jane clapped her hands and said something to her doll.

"C'mon then," Walter said. "Are you sure you're warm enough?"

But Jane was already five paces ahead, her small body buckling with the flood of desire and the breathlessness of grief.

The journey would not be an easy one, for the path down to the sea was treacherous; they would have to hold hands for part of the way, stepping with more courage than faith.

Jane

S HE SAT ON A red towel, looking out to sea. People laden with bags and beach chairs passing slowly across the surface of her Wayfarers. It would soon be time to go home.

The sand beneath her towel had molded to the shape of her body. She glanced down at her legs. They were not as she would have liked them to be, but for her age, she felt she was still attractive. In the deli below her apartment, the Spanish men sometimes flirted with her if they weren't too busy. At the office, she realized that the young girls—the assistants and the interns—probably looked at her as being old. She didn't feel old. Although her feet ached sometimes. Her enthusiasm for life had turned to appreciation for life. And she could feel life getting quieter. *Her* life getting quieter, like the end of a party where only a few people remain at long messy tables, staring at their glasses, at the absent chairs, and at each other.

It was the end of summer and families were migrating back to New York from East Hampton. The lines in the cafés were shorter, and it was no longer difficult to park on Main Street.

In the distance, Jane's teenage daughters sat at the water's edge discussing boys and the secret things known only to siblings.

Jane had been close to her own sister.

They looked very much alike.

And while Jane's accent became unmistakably Irish, her sister had never lost her Canadian twang. They both had blond hair and would take turns twisting braids for one another in the garden on summer days, as their uncle Popsy picked lettuce and whistled.

Jane's daughters were close too.

They were both at the Waldorf School and always ate lunch together. Jane could sense how the world was opening up to her children. The telephone in the kitchen rang all the time now, and their doorman had got to know several boys quite well. Jane approved only of the ones who were nervous when they met her.

Her daughters' lives were very bright; everything felt for the first time.

The roots of her own life had found deep soil—holding her in place. Jane felt the strength and poise to give her children a safe and stable shelter. A place to rest when they sat at the kitchen table and said things that made them cry.

Her children meant everything to her.

The shelter of a mother's love was something that Jane thought of very often, for her own parents had lost their lives in a car accident when she was very little. Then her older sister died of cancer in London two years ago. Jane's husband experienced a breakdown at the funeral and was taken to a hospital in Kings Cross. He had been very fond of her sister.

In Jane's opinion, her sister had never been able to get over the death of their parents, as though a part of her had died too on that long-ago morning when charred debris lay scattered across the freeway outside Toronto.

The first car to come along saw several small fires: Something completely wrong. No trace of people. It was an image Jane conjured daily. Age is a plow that unearths the true nature of things. But only after the moment has passed and we are powerless to change anything, are we granted wisdom. As though we are living backward.

Jane knew her daughters must learn this for themselves, and so there was only one piece of advice Jane wanted to pass on to her girls.

She watched them at the water's edge.

Laughter.

Seagulls swooping down in their endless pursuit of scraps.

The billowing sail of a faraway boat holding the last of the day like a nugget of gold.

One day, Jane thought, this moment will be a long time ago.

———————

For Jane knew that wisdom means knowing when to give everything, knowing exactly the right time to give everything and admit you've done it and not look back. Loving is the path to eternal life, Jane thought, not worship, as she was taught in Ireland.

And she sensed that everyone she had ever touched—whether deeply over years or for only a brief moment in a crowded elevator—might somehow be the whole story of her life.

Jane wiped her eyes and noticed a small child standing at the edge of her blanket with a red bucket.

The girl had lovely eyes. Her belly lunged forward. Her red bucket was full of water. Jane reached out to the girl, but she turned and ran away.

Above her, the sky held on to a few clouds. They hung far out at sea—watching the lives of people who'd gathered at the edge of land.

The red bucket reminded Jane of Walter, calling to her as she reached the edge of the field long ago in Ireland. And then his large, rough hand, which although she didn't know it then, was a young hand.

The beach was dark, and the sand had been packed hard by the outgoing tide. Rain lingered; like something said but not forgotten.

Walter ran to the water's edge, and Jane remembered a moment of panic when he disappeared from her sight—but then he was upon her again. He had found shells and he unloaded them into her small arms.

She told him about her mother and father, and he listened and kissed her once on the forehead, telling her that they would never truly leave her behind—that people, like little fish, are sometimes caught in the cups of rocks as the tide sweeps in and out.

Jane wondered what he meant; whether it was she or her parents who were trapped.

"And should you ever feel too lonely, Jane," Walter said as they carried the moon home in buckets, "listen for the roar of the sea—for in it are all those who've been and all those who are to come."

Jane remembered his words during the long nights in the cottage where she would spend the next fifteen years.

Some nights, she believed that if she listened hard enough, she might hear the voice of her mother and father calling to her from wherever they were.

Some mornings, the moment before she opened her eyes, she had forgotten they were gone; then like all those left behind in the world, Jane would have to begin again. For, despite the accumulation of experience, one must always be ready to begin again, until it's someone else's turn to begin without us, and we are completely free from the pain of love, from the pain of attachment—the price we pay to be involved.

As the sun dropped lazily in the sky, Jane stood and removed her sunglasses. She brushed the sand from her legs. Her eyes were swollen with crying. She stepped across the warm beach down to the water where her daughters were huddled.

When they saw her coming, they made a space and she sat between them—excited and afraid to tell them how the very best and the very worst of life will come from their ability to love strangers.

And they would think she was talking about Dad, about Walter, who grew up in a Gypsy caravan on a cliff, and who every Christmas without fail gives their mother a dozen eggs which he cleans in the sink on Christmas Eve, while they— his two daughters—talk to their friends on the phone, help string the tree with tinsel, or stare out the window at fading shadows, at the happy sadness of yesterday, the promise of tomorrow.

The City of Windy Trees

I

ONE DAY, GEORGE FRACK received a letter. It was from very far away. The stamp had a bird on it. Its wings were wide and still. The bird was soaring high above a forest, its body flecked with red sparks. George wondered if the bird was flying *to* a place or away from it.

At first, George thought the letter had been delivered to him by mistake, but the name on the envelope was his name and the address was where he lived.

Then he opened it and found a page of blue handwriting and a photograph of a little girl with brown hair. The girl was wearing a navy polyester dress dotted with small red hearts. She also had a pink clip in her hair. Her hands were tiny.

The handwriting was full of loops, as if each letter were a cup held fast upon the page by the heaviness of each small intention.

When George read the page, his mouth fell open and a low groaning resounded from his throat.

———————

He held the paper very close to his eyes and read it again several times.

Then he dropped the page and looked around his apartment as though people were watching him from every dusty corner.

On the mantelpiece was the only photograph of his great uncle, Monsieur Saboné, who like George had lived alone in a quiet part of the city where he was born.

George wandered from room to room without knowing why, balancing the words of the letter in his mind; trying to make sense of them.

When George found himself standing in the kitchen, he automatically reached for the teapot. Perhaps because he wasn't himself, he somehow managed to knock it to the floor. When George tried to pick up the pieces, he realized he could not control his shaking hands and he cut his fingers in several places.

Blood dripped onto the broken pieces of china; large spots fell upon the white sink.

George sat on the edge of the bathtub and wrapped his hands in old bandages. He imagined writing out the story of his life across each length of white. What words would he choose; would there be things he wrote that weren't true; would there be spaces for things he wished he had done, people he wanted to meet, but who never came?

George sat on his toilet with the lid down. He remained there for two hours looking at his bandaged hands. When he felt faint, George removed his clothes and slipped into bed. Blood soaked through the bandage and left spots on the sheets.

Outside, a fire engine wailed, changing pitch as it passed: one sound for coming and one for going—the moment in between, indistinguishable.

George was asleep by the time it was dark. Lights went on in kitchens across the city as people arrived home. As George entered his first dream, the unknown world carried on. Men in heavy coats walked dogs outside his front door. Women fell asleep in front of television sets; others stayed up without any good reason. And as in every city, a handful of children gazed gently from windows upon the roads and passageways of their childhood, small questions falling in their minds like a rain that disappears by morning.

When George opened his eyes the next day, they were wet. His body was also very stiff. He unfurled his limbs as though waking from hibernation.

The sky outside his window was very bright. Yellow light fell through holes in the curtain and made patterns on the bed. The patterns came and went with the journey of clouds.

George's first thought was that the whole thing was a dream, but life soon poured over him. On the desk he noticed the tip of the envelope. The photograph of the little girl would be lying next to the letter.

Along the rim of the kitchen sink, George's blood had dried in crimson circles. Pieces of broken teapot on the floor had not moved, like small ruins of an ancient civilization.

George didn't go to work and no one telephoned to see if he was ill.

Every so often he checked the address on the letter to make sure it had been delivered to the right person. Then he looked at the photograph. Then he read the letter again.

He stayed in bed until it was dark and did the very same thing the next day, swallowing mild sleeping pills every few hours and drifting in and out of a slumber heavy with memories from childhood.

In the middle of the night, George woke up sweating and gasping for air. For a few moments, the residue of the dream convinced George he had died and was reliving life all over again—but with the memory of everything that had happened before and all that was going to happen. What would it be like to know every detail of every event that would ever happen? The thought carried him in its arms to another dream.

When George finally woke at noon the next day, he sat up for an hour trying to piece his thoughts together like jigsaw pieces from different puzzles.

When he lay back down and drifted into a snooze, pieces came together by themselves, and the book of his childhood blew open. George heard the sound of his father's key churn the lock of the front door. Home from the office. His suit would be creased from the office chair. A small George sat very still in a room that glowed with the spell of television. He wanted to be found. He wanted to be scooped up like a rock from a river and found precious. And every evening his father returned home, George held his breath, like an understudy watching from the wings. George lived always on the verge of his greatest performance.

Then in the dream, George felt himself reaching for the television, turning up the volume as the shouting got worse. If only they had got divorced. Children at school ripped to pieces by their parents' lack of love, shells of their former selves—and George burning with shame, wanting only to have his parents by themselves in the park on dull after-noons at the duck pond.

Instead, George spent his childhood like a small satellite orbiting their unhappy world.

Then he left home. His parents remained together, until one day his father jumped off the office building where he worked. George imagined his raincoat flapping, then the impact; strangely bent limbs; people circling in disbelief; somebody's ruined day.

George wept at the funeral, not because his father was

dead but because he'd never known him. If grief has levels, this was the one below guilt.

On the third day after receiving the letter, George lay on his back and followed the cracks in the bedroom ceiling with his eyes. He imagined he was on a journey across a tiny Arctic plain.

And then he fell asleep and dreamed it.

At the end of his journey across the snow was the little girl from the photograph, waiting for him in the dress with hearts on it. In the dream, all the hearts were beating. When George drew close, he noticed she had butterfly wings. Whenever he tried to reach her, she fluttered away laughing. The sound of her laughing filled him with joy. George managed to cup the feeling and hold on to it for a few seconds after waking up. In his heart, some tiny piece of what hadn't happened would lodge.

In the afternoon George drank tea in the quiet of his bedroom. He wiped away his blood and took a series of showers, concentrating on a different body part each time. He swept his apartment and threw out many things that at one time had been valuable to him.

On the fifth day, George stared through his bedroom window into backyards of bare trees, children's toys, and half-filled plant pots.

Although he lived on a city avenue, the back room where George spent his evening hours was very quiet. Sometimes a neighbor's dog could be heard barking and scratching weakly at a back door. For some reason, George found these to be comforting sounds—while the mean grinding buses that passed his front room irritated and depressed him.

After graduating from university about ten years ago, George had gradually lost interest in the lives of his friends. He dreaded the blinking red light on his telephone that indicated messages waiting to be heard. He stayed away from gatherings, and he purposefully forgot birthdays. Life had not turned out the way he thought. He had not stayed with the woman he truly loved (she was married and living in Connecticut). His mother died one day at the kitchen table before she could drink her tea. He developed a mysterious pain in his hands. His sister became a single mother to a boy (Dominic) with Down syndrome. His job was uninteresting and he felt that his life was nothing more than a light that would blink once in the history of the universe and then be forgotten.

George had lived for several years without a television. Television made him feel lost and lonely. George's local post office had recently attached one to the wall—an attempt to calm people confined to wait in massive queues. George bought his stamps elsewhere and avoided the voice he felt knew absolutely nothing but refused to stop talking.

Simon Van Booy

George's neighbors were very fond of him, however. His apartment was situated on the top floor of the Greenpoint Home for the Agéd, and George occupied the only dwelling that wasn't part of the "home." It had, of course, originally been built for a live-in nurse, but thanks to a cocktail of modern drugs, the residents had little need for any professional assistance. George could even hear them being intimate, and sometimes the occasional fight, and sometimes sobbing—if he listened with a glass against the wall.

The previous tenant—still discussed in the hallway from time to time when a letter came for him—was a Polish carpenter who punched holes in his walls, then spent half the night repairing them with cutting, sawing, and sanding.

George Frack was not without interests. He liked:

1.   Large Chinese kites
2.   Sitting beside the window in his bathrobe with a box of Raisinets
3.   New-wave European films (viewed only at Eric and Burt's small movie house in Greenpoint)
4.   Horoscopes
5.   Velvet loafers

6.   Drinking coffee in the park from a thermos when nobody was around
7.   His collection of world Snoopy figures (Chinese Snoopy, Arctic Snoopy, Russian Snoopy, Aussie Snoopy, etc. etc.)
8.   David Bowie songs
9.   A cat called Goddard (pronounced God-AR) now deceased
10.   A heavy fall of snow that ruins everyone's plans

George's last serious relationship was with Goddard, a stray cat who one day appeared outside the building and threw himself at everyone who passed. They slept together under the same blanket, and George sometimes awoke to Goddard's paw upon his hand. After almost a year at the Greenpoint Home for the Agéd, Goddard escaped one Sunday morning while George was out buying oranges and sardines. He had squeezed through an open window and carefully stepped down the fire escape.

A few minutes later Goddard lay squashed under a bus. Someone put him in a shoe box; his limp body was like a sack of broken parts.

The evening Goddard died, George stood naked on the edge of his fire escape until it got dark and lights came on one square at a time. Then some neighbor spotted a bare human figure on a fire escape and shouted. Suicide was one thing—but confrontation was out of the question. George climbed back inside. Then he went to bed. His usual supper of Raisinets went untouched. The oranges lay on the floor where they had rolled.

George held the letter and the photograph of the little girl in his hand and sat very quietly in a wooden chair beside his bedroom window. He remembered the feeling of Goddard's head brushing his legs.

After almost a week in his apartment without any human contact, a storm built slowly on the edge of the city and then broke open. George watched from his window as a seamless band of clouds rolled toward him. Trees bent, as if leaned on by invisible hands. The streetlight fell in perfect columns of raindrops.

Cars pulled to the sides of the road. Umbrellas blew out like escaping squid.

George got up from his chair and went to the closet for a blanket. The kitchen light felt good against the darkness of the afternoon. He walked halfway into the kitchen, but then decided against making tea and went back into his bedroom, where he planned on settling down for the night. It was six o'clock.

He sat down and spread the blanket across his legs. He

was wearing his velvet loafers and a bathrobe. The rain tapped gently against the window, magnifying the backyards in long watery lines. The roofs of the buildings glistened black, and a tiny alphabet of birds hung motionless in the sky.

George looked at the photograph. The girl in it would smile forever. Every photograph is a lie, he thought—a splinter from the tree of what happened. Clouds moved from one side of the sky to the other. The darkness would be upon them sooner than ever. George pressed the photograph of the girl to his cheek. In his mind, he could feel her gentle fantasies. Then her heart began to beat within his and he was suddenly full of yearning for this child, a daughter who came in the mail—in a dress of tiny hearts, from a city of windy trees: a place where he had been conjured ten thousand times from a pillow of alternating hope and disappointment.

II

AFTER THE STORM, NIGHT filled the wet city.

George had been still for such a very long time that evening had etched his face into the window before him. It was a face through which city lights twinkled in the windy distance. George leaned forward. The figure before him also leaned, as if ready to hear the whispering of a secret. George imagined his daughter's hands upon his face, like someone blind trying to feel his way around. He wondered what she would make of it.

Would she touch it?

Would she wonder what stories swirled behind the eyes?

Would she find it handsome?

Perhaps she might see herself.

And, then, perhaps in time, it might be a face that she cared for, that she was pleased to see, that gave her comfort in the night when she surfaced on the back of a nightmare.

George ripped open a box of Raisinets and chewed each one carefully. He decided to write a letter to his sister. Since he'd received the photograph of the little girl in the mail, the old love for his sister had stirred; a love that had become buried under the rubble of his life. Growing up, they hadn't said much to one another but sometimes held hands in the car and sometimes cooked together listening to David Bowie after their mother had passed out on the couch, still clutching the neck of a bottle.

One Easter, George left several drawings of rabbits outside her bedroom door. When he found them in the trash can in the kitchen that afternoon, George stormed into her room, grabbed the egg that she was decorating, and stamped on it.

Not until she was a woman did George's sister realize how much her younger brother had looked up to her, and how lonely his life must have been without her friendship. But by that time George had disappeared from her life completely.

George wondered what he would say to her in the letter. He found a pen and some paper from a drawer and sat down at his desk. He went to switch on his lamp, but there was no bulb in it. Then he remembered two boxes of bulbs in the cupboard under the stairs. He went to fetch one.

Several weeks ago, while walking home from work, George passed what he thought was a shop. In the window were packs of diapers, dusty toys in sun-bleached boxes, a pile of women's clothes, and three dirty boxes of lightbulbs, which reminded George that he needed some.

When he tried to enter the shop, however, he found the door locked. As he stepped back to see if the opening times had been posted, a panel opened in the door and a face appeared.

"Yeah?" the face said.

"How much are those lightbulbs?" George asked.

The face eyed him suspiciously.

"What lightbulbs?" the face said.

"The lightbulbs in the window—how much are they?"

The face tightened as if agitated and then disappeared, leaving the panel open.

A moment later, the face returned. It stared curiously at George Frack.

"So how much are they?" George asked.

The face laughed.

"A dollar," the face said.

"Each or for the pack?"

"For the pack."

"Great," George said. "I'll take two packs."

"Okay," the face said, "that's two dollars."

"What about tax?" George asked.

"Okay, that's two dollars and nineteen cents," the face said, and laughed again.

A week later, the shop was raided by the police and then boarded up by city workers with cigarettes in their mouths.

George found the two boxes of lightbulbs in his closet under the stairs where he had set them. He put one in the lamp on his desk.

It came to life before he had finished screwing it in.

Then he began the letter to his sister.

She was a single mother to a boy named Dominic with Down syndrome. George had not spoken to her since Dominic was born. All George knew was that his nephew was conceived one night on a skiing holiday in Canada with a man who had another family. As George wrote his sister's name, he realized that Dominic would have no idea who he was.

Dear Helen,

I know I haven't written to you before like this
~~before~~- but I wanted to tell you that I'm going to
Sweden. I also want to explain that the reason I
haven't kept in touch is because I felt sorry that
your life was ruined.

This afternoon I sat by the window and watched
the rain. I was thinking about my life--but not in the
usual way. I don't think I feel sorry for you anymore,
Helen, or for us for that matter.

While I sit here*-life is going on without me.

If not for something that happened to me a few
days ago, I would not have realized that your life with
Dominic--while being hard at times--is probably full of a
joy we never had as kids.

One day soon I will come and visit you.

Is this okay?

You will see my headlights in the driveway. I will
bring food in white plastic bags from the supermarket.
Perhaps the three of us might cook something together,

...the way we did when we were little. I can't say
it tasted very good, but that ~~want~~ wasn't the point,
and don't you think the quality of food is higher since
the advent of those automatic sprinkler systems in the
produce aisle?

     I can't tell you when I will see you, but it will
be before the end of the year.

     There's something I have to do first--somewhere I
have to go, someone I have to meet, and someone I have
to become.

I am the most important person to someone I didn't
even know existed.

Wish me luck...
Your Brother,

~~-George-~~ MAJOR TOM

p.s. for some reason I think my passport is in the boxes of
    Mom's things that you have. Would you send it to me as
    soon as possible? MORE THAN ONE LIFE DEPENDS ON THIS.

p.p.s. I had a cat--but it was killed by a bus. I wish he
    had met Dominic--they could have played together.

p.p.p.s. I regret things I haven't done--rahter than thing[S]I
    have--strange eh?

~~--p.p.p..p.p-~~ FINAL NOTE: Do you still like David Bowie?

    ENCL: Two Boxes of Raisinets

Then George crossed out his name, and wrote "Major Tom."

A few days later, Human Resources from George's office called. They kept calling him Mr. Frack. George asked them to call him George, but they wouldn't. There were two people talking on the same line, and at various points in the conversation, nobody knew who was talking to whom. George kept looking down at his velvet loafers. After ten minutes, George's boss came on the line. It sounded like he was chewing. He was a boorish man from the suburbs who picked his nose when he didn't think anyone was looking.

George said he didn't understand why they had called. His boss asked George if he was kidding. Then he told George that he was being fired. George sighed.

"Well, that's fine," George said, "because I'm going to Sweden for a while."

There was silence, and then his boss said:

"Where the hell is Sweden?"

"It's like Scandinavia—or something," George said, looking for an open pack of Raisinets.

A week later, his passport arrived. In the package was:

1. A pair of adult-sized mittens
2. A kid's drawing of a whale with "Good Luck!" written on it in blue and yellow crayon
3. A letter from his sister
4. A list of things they had cooked when they were children
5. One of three drawings secretly rescued from the trash after the egg incident

The letter from his sister was addressed to "Major Tom" and signed "Ground Control."

A short P.S. read: "You've really made the grade."

III

G EORGE'S TAXI BROKE DOWN on the way to the airport. The driver cursed in Hindi, then ripped a tiny
plastic deity from the dashboard and yelled into its face.

George leaned forward and explained to the driver that
he had a daughter he'd never met, that she was waiting for
him, that he had only one chance to find her. The driver
replaced the deity with a kiss, then threw open his door and
ran out onto the Brooklyn-Queens Expressway, waving his
arms. George noticed that he was wearing loafers—patent
leather.

Several cars skidded, almost hitting a Wonder Bread
truck. The bread truck driver jumped from the cab and
stood with his chest against the taxi driver's face. The cars
behind suddenly stopped honking. Just when it seemed the
truck driver was going to punch the taxi driver, the two
men shook hands. The cars behind started honking again.

George climbed into the bread truck. A small Puerto
Rican flag dangled from the rearview mirror. The driver
swerved in and out of traffic as though sewing up the highway. He smoked one cigarette after another. A can of Red
Bull fell from the cup holder and spilled all over George's
velvet loafers. The driver laughed. George could hear the
bread flying around in the back, hitting the sides with dull
thumps.

When they arrived at Newark International Airport, the driver looked at George and shouted, "Go, motherfucker, go."

George grabbed his bag and fell from the cab, then sprinted through the doors into the terminal.

The woman at check-in had a glass eye. She told George he had five minutes to get to the gate. Then a large African-American man in gold-rimmed glasses studded with fake diamonds appeared on an airport golf cart. He told George to climb on, and they beeped their way to the gate, scattering passengers on all sides.

Once at a cruising altitude, the passengers around George began to sleep—like people falling into pools of their own lives.

George thought about his journey to the airport. He'd never see those men again. Love between strangers takes only a few seconds and can last a whole life.

Then he thought back six years to the night he'd spent with the Swedish hotel clerk at a truck stop in upstate New York; it was the night of beginning, because it was the only night they were together. To think that one unplanned night with a stranger in a strange place could create the most precious person who ever lived.

———————

Six years ago, George had a sort of nervous breakdown. Instead of calling an ambulance and waiting on the couch in his underwear, George decided he was going to drive to his ex-girlfriend's wedding in Massachusetts and then charge the cake as it was brought out. He pictured himself being arrested and then institutionalized. He imagined the pleasure of sitting in a bathrobe on a bench beside a rose garden, nurses gliding past like swans.

The wedding was to take place on a Saturday morning. George left on Friday and drove until his nerves could no longer handle the traffic. He took the next exit and followed the car in front. He wondered who was in it, what sort of life they were having. He knew he would never see their face and that their lights would soon disappear along the road to somewhere he could not imagine.

Then George spotted a red neon sign:

RED'S, SINCE 1944.

He parked and went inside.

The waitresses wore white shirts with frilly collars and black vests. There were plastic flowers on all the tables. The wind howled against the windows.

Opposite the diner, about half a mile in the distance, burned the lights of a correctional facility.

There were photographs of 1950s baseball players on the

walls. Snow blew around the parking lot. A storm had been predicted, and the waitresses kept looking through the windows and pointing.

The silverware was flimsy. George bent his spoon with one hand. The spoon reminded George of a child's hand.

The lamp shades hung low over each table. George asked for the special. When he finished his glass of Diet Coke, the waitress brought another, but George's mouth was so full of bread, he could only nod when she set it down on the table before him.

A man walked his little son to the bathroom. They were both wearing neckties. The boy kept touching his. Near the entrance was a lobster tank with only one lobster in it. George wondered what the lobster was thinking; perhaps wondering when the others were coming back.

When George returned from the bathroom, his food had arrived. The lobster tank was empty. George ate a few mouthfuls painfully, and then concentrated on the coleslaw which lay in a sad heap half off the plate.

Outside, snow lay thick upon the picnic tables. A couple at the next table was eating dinner. They were about George's age. They were wearing scarves and laughing. They ordered a bottle of wine, and it arrived with a napkin around its neck. Why did everyone else's life seem perfect?

At the other end of the restaurant, a father held his daughter aloft, as though he had just pulled her from the ground. George felt dizzy. There were plastic snowflakes hanging in the windows.

George tipped the waitress the year of his ex-girlfriend's birthday, $19.72—more than the meal itself.

He knew he was only twenty minutes from where the wedding was being held the next day, so when George saw a sign for lodging not far from the restaurant, he followed the flashing arrow. The hotel was a line of connected chalets, each with the same color door. Lines of trucks filled the parking lot, their engines like snouts gleaming and puffing in the moonlight.

Drivers milled about, smoking and stomping the snow from their boots.

The check-in desk was lit by a long fluorescent bulb missing its cover. An ashtray on the counter was full of ash but no cigarette butts. There was also a calendar with a glossy photograph of a Mack truck.

George rang the bell and waited. Nobody came.

As he turned to leave, a woman with short black hair appeared.

"Sorry," she said.

"It's okay," George said.

Her skin was pockmarked, but her eyes were very beautiful. Her hair was uneven, as though she'd cut it herself. She also had an accent. When she spoke, it sounded like she was singing.

"A room?" she asked.

"Yes, please," George said.

"Are you a driver?" she said, looking at her book.

George thought for a moment and remembered all the rigs parked outside.

"No," he said, "just a regular person."

The woman laughed.

"245," she said. "It's on the second floor. How do you wish to pay?"

George handed her his credit card.

"Nonsmoking—is that all right?"

"I don't smoke," George said.

The woman looked at his credit card and said his name aloud.

"George Frack."

"Yes," George said.

"That's a funny name."

"Is it?"

"It sounds like it's made up."

"Well, it's not made up," George said. "I've had it for years."

"Well, here's your key, George Frack."

George took his key and thanked her. Then, for some reason, instead of going immediately to his room and getting into bed as he'd planned, he turned to her and said:

"Where are you from—I like your voice."

The woman stared at him closely.

"Sweden."

"Oh," George said, "so you're happy about the snow."

"I am," she said.

"What are you doing here?"

"You mean, working at a truck stop in Nowhere, New York?"

"Yes."

"It's a long sad story, George Frack. Why are you here?"

"It's a long sad story also."

A trucker passed through the lobby and disappeared into the bar, leaving a trail of cigarette smoke.

"Do you want to watch TV with me in my room later?" George said.

"Okay," the woman answered without looking up. "I'll be over in two hours—shall I bring anything?"

"Orange juice, please."

"And how about some Raisinets?" she said.

"Candy?" George said.

"You'll see."

An hour later, Marie sat with George on his bed. The room was quite sad. Cigarette burns in the carpet, a ball of sweatpants in a drawer, dirty ashtrays, the cap from a bottle of something under the bed.

Instead of watching television, Marie told George about

how she'd come to New York to find her father. Her mother said he was a truck driver—at least he was in 1978.

"You picked a good spot," George said.

"I suppose so," she said.

"How long have you been here?"

"Almost three months—but I'm going back next week because my visa runs out."

"You didn't find him then?"

"I hoped I'd recognize him."

"At least you tried."

Marie shook some Raisinets into George's hand.

"My father is dead," George said.

"Is that why you're so unhappy?"

George thought for a moment. "Actually yes," he said.

"But why are you up here, George Frack?"

"I don't think I know anymore," George said, moving deeper under the covers. Then Marie kissed him.

Afterward, they lay in each other's arms without saying anything.

When George woke up the next morning, Marie was gone. The bed was full of Raisinets. He'd missed the wedding. The television was a reflection of the room. He took a shower, then got in his car and drove home. The traffic was very light.

IV

WHEN GEORGE'S PLANE TOUCHED down in Stockholm, it was still dark. Orange Volvo wagons idled within yellow lines painted around the docked aircraft.

A group of men stood about a luggage cart looking up at the faces that peered out from the small windows of the airplane. Some of the men wore blue headsets around their necks.

A child started to cry.

George thought the man next to him was asleep, but then he reached up and touched his mustache, as if to check that George hadn't stolen it.

As people made their way lugubriously to passport control, George noticed that the man who'd been sitting next to him was limping badly. He was soon passed by all the other passengers. Three mechanics glided by on small scooters.

The woman in the passport booth hardly looked at George's passport. Then he was suddenly waiting for his luggage. He recognized a few faces from the plane. Most of the passengers were Swedish and talked quietly in singsong voices.

He couldn't believe he'd done it, that he was a father—that he was in Sweden. A situation George would have thought nightmarish if it had been put to him hypothetically was now the single most important thing that had ever happened to him.

Life had called his name, and without thinking, he had stepped forward. He wondered if perhaps he was becoming the person he had always wanted to be.

On the plane, George had made a list of the different jobs he might enjoy and that might earn him enough to travel back and forth to Sweden. Maybe he might even live in Sweden. He liked snow, after all, and he owned a green Saab.

A little girl sat on the edge of the baggage car, dangling her feet as though she were on the edge of a pier on the last day of her family vacation. Her eyes kept closing and then opening. Several more children arrived and did the same thing—sat on the edge of an empty baggage cart and dangled their legs off.

The baggage area was bright but desolate. People watched the pushing belt of suitcases and boxes. George sat on his briefcase as though it were a very small horse. The only things in it were the photograph of the little girl, a photograph of Goddard, the stuff from his sister, plus several boxes of Raisinets.

For the first time, George wished he'd held on to the money his mother left him when she died. What wasn't used to pay off debts, George had spent on thirty pairs of velvet loafers and delicate kites from China—of which not a single one remained. Of the thirty-seven kites he'd bought through the mail, about two dozen had ripped when George

launched them from the New Jersey cliffs. Others had broken in mid-flight and dotted the trees of McCarren Park.

It had occurred to George that if his plane crashed, one
reason might be that one of his missing kites had landed on
the windshield as they tried to take off.

Everyone had collected their luggage and seemed to be
walking in one direction. George followed. If there was a
customs, George wasn't aware that he'd walked through it.
He followed several knots of passengers down an escalator
to a train platform. He felt as though he was quite deep
underground, as above the tracks the ceiling seemed to be
natural rock. There was not a single piece of litter on the
platform, and George could hear the low buzzing of the
neon sign that announced the time of the next depart-
ing train. The announcement was made in Swedish, then
English.

At the station in central Stockholm, George got some
money from an ATM, called a Bankomat.

With thousands of kronor in his pocket—and knowing
nothing about how much meant anything—George joined
the line of people waiting for taxis. There was a large man
in a yellow jumpsuit directing people into cabs, which were
all Volvos. There was a woman in a wheelchair in front
of George who had to sit to one side while the dispatcher
waited for a different kind of taxi. George wondered why
someone couldn't pick her up and carry her into the car. He

even thought of volunteering, but perhaps the only man allowed to carry her was her husband.

The taxi driver had a large head and thin white hair. He wore a black leather jacket that read "Taxi 150000" on the arm. He also had thick silver hoops in both ears.

At the hotel, the woman at reception informed George that he wouldn't be able to check in until 2 PM. When he sighed, she asked if he wanted to leave his luggage and go for some breakfast. It was about ten o'clock, and the sky was beginning to brighten.

As he walked along the street, it started to rain. It was light and refreshing, but then it got heavy and George was soon quite wet. He walked and walked, looking for somewhere to have coffee but passed only offices.

He wished for someone to stop him and talk. He wanted to say that it was his first day in Sweden and that he had come to see his daughter.

George wondered if it was a custom for offices at street level to have large clear windows, because they all did.

Every so often, George stopped and looked in on a board meeting or a secretary who had changed under her desk from heels to flats. Through one large window, George stood for some time in the pouring rain and watched a pretty woman with her hair tied in a bun. She was brushing the frame of an old mirror. On a shelf behind her was a small microwave with black finger marks, heaviest around the door.

When George saw a woman with a shopping bag that read "NationalMuseet" on the side, he walked in the direction from which she had come, hoping that he might find a museum where he could dry off and sit down for a while. Everything seemed to be closed.

For several hours, George simply walked around in the rain. He had never been so wet and so cold. When he finally checked into his hotel room, he took a hot bath, then sat on his bed in the hotel bathrobe. He dried his feet and held his velvet loafers under the hair dryer for half an hour.

He took the letter from his pocket and looked at the address. The area of Stockholm where she lived was called Södermalm.

He picked up the phone and dialed the number as it was written on the letter. A child answered.

"Hello?" George said.

"*Hej,*" the small voice said.

Then a few seconds of silence.

"Ma-ma," the voice said, and George heard the echo of footsteps. The woman on the other end of the line repeated her phone number in Swedish.

"It's George," George said.

"George?" the voice said.

"George Frack."

There was a faint gasp and then silence.

"Was that her?" George asked.

Just when George was about to repeat the question, he realized the woman was crying.

He heard the child say something gentle to her mother in Swedish.

"I didn't expect you to come to Sweden," Marie said.

"I know," George said.

Then Marie said something to the child, which met with a few words of protest.

"I just told her to go and wait for me in her bedroom," Marie said quietly, "because I'm going to beg you, George Frack—don't come here if it's only to see what she looks like."

"I know what she looks like," George said, glancing down at his briefcase.

"Oh," Marie said.

"Does she know who I am?"

"No," Marie said. "Though she asks me every day why she doesn't have a daddy."

"And what do you say?"

"I said nothing, until two weeks ago, when I said that you worked in America."

"Is that when you wrote to me?" George asked.

"Yes, George Frack—do you remember why?"

"Yes," George said. "Funny how we do what was done to us."

Silence again.

"After I told her, she began putting up pictures of President Bush all over her bedroom, and I realized that I had made a terrible mistake. I should have told you at the beginning."

"I'm not mad," George said quickly.

"Her name is Charlotte."

"I want her to know me," George said.

"She doesn't know you," Marie said. "And she already loves you."

Then she started crying again.

"Are you married, Marie?"

"I'm engaged. And you are married with kids I suppose, George Frack?"

"No," George said. "But I had a cat."

"You'll meet my fiancé. He's nice, quite a bit older than me—twenty years, actually. He was the one who encouraged me to write to you."

"Really? What's his name?"

"Philip."

"He sounds nice," George said.

"Can you give me a few hours to think, George? I know it's a lot to ask, but—"

"Sure. I'm staying at the Hotel Diplomat—call me when you're ready."

George hung up and lay back on his bed. He took a box of Raisinets from his briefcase and ate a handful. He then found a large envelope with the hotel name on it. In the envelope, George put his boarding pass, the chocolate he'd found balancing on his pillow, a feather that had been in his jacket pocket for years, a small thin bar of soap from the bathroom, and a drawing he'd done on the plane—of the man with the mustache.

Then George took a blue pen from the desk and wrote "Dominic Frack" on the paper. Then his sister's address.

He sat on his bed and turned the television on. Then he turned it off again.

He picked up the phone and dialed his sister's number, making sure he pressed the country code in first.

It rang and rang and rang.

George wondered if Helen was giving Dominic a bath. He imagined himself standing next to her with a towel. Dominic's shiny face. Clouds against the window. Trees outside too, and the sea not far away.

A few minutes later, the phone rang of its own accord.

"George," Marie said, "I don't want to wait because I'm afraid you'll change your mind and it will be my fault."

"Good," George said.

"Meet us at Skansen in two hours—it's a park with animals, not far from your hotel."

"Is it still raining?" George said.

"No, George, look outside."

Outside, flakes the size of buttons drifted down and settled upon the earth. People on the sidewalks had slowed to look.

Then in the background, George heard his daughter scream something in Swedish.

"Did she just say it's snowing?" George asked.

Within a couple of hours, the snow had stopped, leaving a thin layer of white across the city—just enough to catch footprints and bicycle tracks.

George took a shower. Then he shaved and brushed his teeth. He slowly dressed in his finest suit. Then he put on a brand-new pair of velvet loafers he'd brought with him. There were balls of tissue paper in the toes.

George left his hotel and walked east along the Strandvägen toward the bridge. After crossing the busy road, he came to a fork. One path held the painted outline of an adult and child walking hand in hand; the other had the painted outline of a bicycle.

It was very cold outside, and each time George exhaled, he passed through a cloud of his own life.

Skansen was a park within a park. The Djurgården, in which the park was situated, was once the king's private hunting grounds. Joggers passed in yellow spandex and thick hats. Along the water there were many boats. George guessed that they took tourists to the small, uninhabited islands around Stockholm. Most were closed for the winter, though one boat had lights on around its deck. As George approached, he saw several men working on the deck with their tools laid out next to them. As he passed, one of the men said something and waved. George smiled and waved back.

George entered the park through a blue iron arch with gold deer heads carved at the top. Birds swung from tree to tree. The path took him along the edge of another small lake. George checked the trees for the wreckage of kites. He wished he'd brought one. Ducks glided along the banks, while farther out, tall white birds cried out in the mist that lingered upon the surface of the lake.

When he reached the entrance to Skansen, George found that he was the only person there. A man with silver-rimmed glasses waved to him from the ticket office. George approached.

"One adult ticket?" the man asked.

"No, three tickets," George said. "I'm expecting a woman

and a girl in an hour—and I'd like to pay for them too."

The man looked a little confused. "How will I know if they're the right people?"

"I don't know," George said.

"Is it your family?" the man said helpfully.

George nodded.

"Then I'll look out for a girl who looks like you."

George nodded and grinned a little.

"There are also two other entrances," the man added, "so if they don't come through my gate, come back before we close and I'll refund your money."

"Okay, I will," George said.

"Where are you meeting them?" the man asked.

"Somewhere, I guess." George said.

"Very good," the man said. "Well, I should tell you that Skansen was founded by Artur Hazelius in 1891."

"1891?" George said.

"I think you're going to be surprised."

"I think I'm already surprised," George said.

"That's what we like to hear," the man said. He was a cheerful sort of person.

George walked through the deserted model town that was supposed to be a miniature Sweden. There were empty workshops, empty schools, empty shops that in summer would be full of employees in period costume and Swedish children licking ice creams.

In the middle of winter, Skansen was like George's life: a world that quietly waited for people to fill it.

After a few minutes, George's loafers were covered in snowy mud. Birds circled high above the park. As he passed a plowed square of soil with a sign that read "Herbgarden," George found himself on a ridge overlooking the city of Stockholm. The sound of cars and trains echoed through the cold air as a continuous hum, broken only by the occasional call of a bird from faraway trees.

When George approached the aviary, he noticed an empty stroller. A few yards away, a small woman was holding a girl up to the bars so she could see. George looked at his watch. He wasn't supposed to meet them for another hour. As he approached, the little girl turned around as if she sensed him.

George stood still.

He looked at the girl and she looked back at him. She was the first to smile. It was the face from the photograph.

Then her mother turned and looked at George. She slipped a handkerchief from her sleeve and wiped her eyes.

"Hello," George said. But though his mouth moved, the word came out so quietly that only he heard it.

"Hello, George Frack," Marie said.

She looked much older than George remembered. Her

body sagged in the middle, and her hair was flat and thin. But her eyes were still beautiful.

"*Vem är han?*" Charlotte said to her mother.

"*Han är George,*" her mother said. "*Talar engelska, Lotta.*"

"Hello," Charlotte said, turning to George. "My name is Lotta."

"My name is George."

"Would you like to come with us, George?" Lotta said.

George fought to control the trembling in his throat.

"I'd like that," he said.

And so, as Marie watched from a little way off, Lotta took George's cold, shaky hand into her little hot hand and led him through the aviary.

"The houses here are from all over Sweden," Lotta said. "There are many wild animals too and an owl—two owls."

"Really," George said.

"What's your favorite animal, Mr. George?"

"Cats."

"Me also!" Lotta exclaimed.

Before they reached the owl enclosure, George felt dizzy. Then his legs crumpled beneath him, and he lay motionless in the mud looking up at clouds.

Lotta stood and watched, unsure of what to do. Marie rushed over. The sound of footsteps on wet earth, then

George sobbing so loud that some of the animals turned to see from their cages.

After that, Lotta kept her distance from George, though every so often she would hand him a piece of candy covered in pocket-dust.

Later on, as a family of bored elk chewed straw, Lotta took George's hand again.

"Are you okay, Mr. George?" she said.

"No," George said. "I'm actually pretty freaked out."

Then Marie knelt down and held Lotta by her shoulders. The elk continued chewing behind them.

"*Lotta, George är dina pappa.*"

Lotta looked up at George.

Then her face broke apart.

"*George är dina pappa, Lotta,*" Marie shouted, shaking Lotta as if she were a lifeless doll.

George looked down at his fingers.

Lotta screamed and ran away.

Her mother shouted for her to come back.

Then George, without consciously deciding to, began to chase her. He could feel the mud splashing up his legs. He felt dizzy again, but his legs moved faster than he'd ever imagined. In the distance, a small figure rounded a corner. George followed it. He caught sight of her again, her brown hair tossed with each desperate stride. When he caught up to her, he reached out for her shoulders and they both fell into the snowy mud.

George grabbed her and held her close. He rocked her back and forth and their bodies dug a small space in the earth to cradle their weight.

An employee feeding the animals watched and then turned away with a sigh.

When Lotta reached her arms around George's neck, he could feel the heat of her mouth against his cheek. It was the weight of the entire world pressed against him in two small lips.

Even when Marie appeared, breathless—they wouldn't let go of one another.

Lotta's hair smelled like apples.

And her hands were so very small.

They left the park in darkness. The moon hung above the city like a bare knuckle. Water clapped against heavy boats and then, encircling Stockholm, re-created a city of no consequences.

Lotta was singing loudly in her stroller. She held the flag George had bought her at the museum shop. It had a cat on it.

Lotta kept turning to look at George; but her small face was hidden by shadows. George imagined her blinking eyes, her small hands under the blanket, hot breaths, the feeling of being pushed along the muddy path home.

V

A FEW DAYS LATER, ICE-SKATING at the Kung-
strädgården. Lotta is doing pirouettes on the ice. It is
late. They ate dinner at Max—Lotta's favorite hamburger
restaurant. After eating a third of her burger, Lotta had a
Blizzer. She said it was very sweet, and she made George
try a few mouthfuls with a flimsy spoon. Marie's boyfriend,
Philip, joined them when he finished work. He sells home
appliances. Philip's wife left him in 1985 for another man
with whom she now lives in Gothenburg. Philip's daughter is grown up and goes to university. Lotta likes to tease
Philip by running away with his hat.

The man who served them at Max Hamburger was
cross-eyed, so no one in the line knew whom he was
talking to. Lotta thought this was funny, even when the
man glared at her (if he was glaring at her). The restaurant had orange doors. Tired fathers drank coffee; shopping bags balanced on the end bars of strollers. On the
wall were photographs charting the pictorial history of
Max Hamburger.

The outdoor ice-skating rink was not far from the restaurant. Clouds rubbed faintly against an early evening sky.
In the distance burned the bright neon letters of the Sven-
ska Handelsbanken.

The streetlights were a cluster of white balls, with a

single dome of light held aloft. Many of the buildings were painted yellow.

George had never ice-skated before. Lotta pulled him around the statue that stood in the middle of the small rink watching over everything but seeing nothing.

"We're on the top of the world," Lotta shouted. "This is the North Pole!"

Marie and Philip watched from the side, their arms locked.

Then George broke away and began to skate clumsily but without falling over.

"Look at Pappa," Lotta shouted. And George knew that he had to keep going, despite the feeling that at any moment he might slip or the ground under his feet might suddenly be taken away—he had to stay up, he had to keep moving, and in time he would learn how to do it.

VI

WHEN THE COLD AT the ice rink became too much,
George and Lotta changed back into their shoes,
and they all found a café in which to warm up.

The city was cold and quiet but with lights everywhere.

There will be many things to sort out. George, Philip, and
Marie will spend many nights drinking schnapps talking
about arrangements. The four of them are convinced things
can work out.

Lotta has stopped wetting her bed. She wonders what
New York looks like. She wonders if she will ever look down
from a skyscraper at all the people. She has put a photo
of Goddard next to her bedside lamp. Her favorite David
Bowie song is "Life on Mars?"

On the subway back to Lotta's house in Södermalm, Lotta
tells George about the old boat that was found in Stockholm
harbor.

She tells him how in 1628, the most beautiful ship ever
made sank before it could get out to sea. And then over three

hundred years later, somebody decided to find it and bring it back to life.

Lotta wants to know if they have museums in New York. George tells her there are many. She asks if there is a cat museum. George tells her that he wishes there were one.

Then he thinks about the idea of a museum: the physical record of things; the history of miracles; the miracle of nature and the miracle of hope and perseverance, arranged in such a way as to never be forgotten, or lost, or simply mistaken for everyday things with no particular significance.

Acknowledgments

Beverly Allen; Amy Baker; Bryan Le Boeuf; Darren and Raha Booy; Mrs. J. E. Booy; Dr. Stephen Booy; Douglas Borroughs Esq.; Milan Bozic; Ken Browar; David Bruson; Gabriel Byrne; Le Château Frontenac in Quebec City; Justine Clay; Mary Beth Constant; Christine Corday; Donald Crowhurst; Dr. Silvia Curado; Jennifer Dorman; Cathy Erway; Danielle Esposito; Patricio Ferrari; Peggy Flaum; Dr. Giovanni Frazzetto; Pippo and Salvina Frazzeto; Léon and Hélène Garcia; Colin Gee; Joel Gotler; Lauren Gott; Dr. Greg Gulbransen; Audrey Harris; Dr. Maryhelen Hendricks; Nancy Horner; Mr. Howard; Lucas Hunt; Tim Kail; Carrie Kania; Alan Kleinberg; Hilary Knight; Claude Lelouch; Eva Lontscharitsch; Little M; Alain Malraux; Lisa Mamo; Michael Matkin; McNally Jackson Booksellers; Dr. Bob Milgrom; Dr. Edmund Miller; Carolina Moraes; Cal Morgan; Jennifer Morris; Samuel Morris III; Bill Murray; Dr. William Neal; Ermanno Olmi; Lukas Ortiz; Jonathan Rabinowitz; Nonno Nina and Nonna Lucia Ragaglia; Alberto Rojas; Russo Family of Morano Calabro, Italy; Leah Schachar; Stephanie Selah; Ivan Shaw; Michael Signorelli; Philip Spitzer; Jessamyn Tonry; F.C.V., Eve K. Tremblay; Wim Wenders; Dr. Barbara Wersba.

About the author

About the book

Read on

P.S.

Insights,
Interviews
& More . . .

Meet Simon Van Booy

© 2008 by Ken Browar

MY PUBLISHER has asked me to tell you a little about my life. And I *want* to tell you about my life, but whenever I start writing about myself, I stop to wonder:

Did this actually happen?

Or am I imagining it?

And then the bits I've written that I think are true—I read them over and say to myself: "How could that possibly have happened, Simon? You were three."

And so I delete it and return to the beauty of a blank page.

So as an alternative, I have been trying to write about things I know *definitely* happened (e.g., getting lost on a ferry; sharpening sticks in a cow field with my pen knife; getting

> 66 I have been trying to write about things I know *definitely* happened . . . 99

bullied), but I have written myself into another corner:

When in the middle of the memory that I'm remembering (and writing about), I suddenly leave the path at some moment of ambiguity and find myself writing a story. And I find that only in the world of a story am I able to capture my true feelings about life in a way I could NEVER reveal if I were simply writing a chronological account of what literally happened.

(As I write this, I'm eating soup out of a mixing bowl with a teaspoon, and as I feared—the spoon has fallen in.)

So when Carrie (publisher of HarperPerennial) asked me to write this section, "About the author," I realized that I've already done it— and with such unplanned sincerity (through my stories) that to write what I thought had happened to me would be nothing more than an attempt to make contact with you.

But I hope we're past that.

I hope that each story you read was a meal we sat down to without talking. ❧

How to Find a Story

Now in this section try shutting me up (you won't be able to).

I wish to take you behind the scenes of a story. I've packed sandwiches and tea for us. A small rowing boat with two plaid blankets bobs on the outgoing tide … so c'mon.

How to Find a Story

I go somewhere (generally in winter when tourism lulls) with no idea whatsoever for a story. Then after I'm settled into a hotel, I begin walking the streets. Sometimes I walk all day—sometimes all night, sometimes in the rain (Stockholm for "The City of Windy Trees"), sometimes heat (Las Vegas for "The Missing Statues"), and occasionally in heavy snow (Quebec City for "Love Begins in Winter"). This is one of the most enjoyable parts to building a story because the key is NOT to look for a story but to simply be open to the idea of wandering around and just lingering—like a peculiar odor.

It's always a mystery to people why I choose the places I choose to visit— but it's also a mystery to me. Think of a pin, a map, and a blindfold.

I am a decadent *flâneur* and have no preconceived idea of what I wish to see. Once in Paris, I went into McDonald's for a shake and fries and was struck with the feeling I would need to write *that* Paris story ("Little Birds"). I had already picked my characters from an incident I witnessed on the Métro—but I would need a "feeling" to bring the characters to life, and I found it while eating French fries.

My stories live in places you'd never dream of looking for them—like McDonald's in Paris, or a shoe repair shop in Brooklyn, or a dusty toy shop in Rome with a window display that's faded beyond recognition.

For a place to yield a story, I must travel to it alone, always alone. If I am to meet a friend there, it must be someone who will allow me to be alone and who understands the need for silence and total secrecy. All writers live a secret life. All writers are spies. Sometimes I won't begin the story until I return home, but on my trip I've harvested details and followed my characters. Only in solitude do I realize the true value of life. Only in solitude do I look around and realize what's most important.

In 2006 I went to a tiny village in Italy called Morano Calabro to find a story. The village was hard to find. I traveled there alone but had to ▶

> 66 My stories live in places you'd never dream of looking for them . . . 99

meet the relatives of a friend because they were lending me a small house to live and work in. My friend had asked them to leave me alone while I was in the village, and they agreed they would, but I think they found it a bit suspicious. I have to be honest and say that if they hadn't left me alone, I would never have been able to write the story "The Still but Falling World." What I appreciated very much were the small packages I would find on my doorstep some evenings. Inside would be a delicious meal, usually still hot. In Italy, people will cook for you whether you like it or not, and whether they like *you* or not. I often have to force myself to be alone—while at other times it feels very natural.

Another thing that happened in Morano Calabro that had a major influence on the story was how the children of the village wanted so desperately to play. In the late afternoons, I would be sitting at my desk before an open window that looked down on the street. One afternoon a ball of paper flew in through the window and landed on my desk. It had a drawing of a ship on it, and in childish writing it said (in Italian), "What are you doing in there?"

66 In Italy, people will cook for you whether you like it or not, and whether they like *you* or not. 99

6

I wrote something underneath and threw it out the window.

I heard little shoes scurrying on the cobbles below, and then a child's voice say (in Italian):

"Where's the pen gone?"

Within a few minutes I received a reply, and thus a little ritual was born. It usually lasted until the crowd of children had swelled to a number large enough to alert some old grandmother, who came outside with a broom and chased them away from my window.

From that experience, I felt the heart of the story begin to beat. The story would be built on the desperately beautiful truth that children love their parents with blind passion—no matter what they (the parents) have done. I think in some ways, it's children who need to teach adults—or at least remind us of things that are lost within us.

Also in that village, people fill empty plastic bottles with water and put them on their doorsteps. Someone told me that it supposedly deters dogs or cats (I forget which) from relieving themselves on the step. A year later, in 2007, I was on a car journey with my aunt Margaret who lives in a suburb of Dublin. ▶

I was telling her about Italy and must have mentioned this anecdote. Very recently, my mother called me after returning from Dublin to describe a peculiar incident involving her sister, Margaret—that she has filled her garden with twenty-plus clear plastic bottles full of water—on account of how she passionately believes that it stops cats and dogs from peeing on the grass. My mother said she couldn't imagine who would have suggested such a thing.

When I travel somewhere, I'm also trying to engage with the *feeling* of the place. This is usually a collaboration with how I'm feeling at that time. Stockholm in winter was the perfect city for George Frack because the days are very short and somehow hopeless, as George's life was before he knew about Lotta. But the character came after I'd visited the city. So I suppose I should say George was perfect for Stockholm and not the other way around.

Another detail about "The City of Windy Trees" is that in Stockholm I stayed at the Diplomat Hotel and actually wrote the story there (I still have my room key). And like poor George when he arrives at the hotel, I was not allowed to go to my room

66 Stockholm in winter was the perfect city for George Frack because the days are very short and somehow hopeless, as George's life was before he knew about Lotta. 99

until the official check-in time in the afternoon, which was eight hours away. So I was forced to walk around in the rain for hours and hours, until a curator at the National Museum, a dark-haired girl with very short hair took pity on me and told me to check my wet coat and have hot coffee in the café, which I did. This museum is very interesting—if you ever have a chance to visit—and the staff was very kind to me.

In "The Missing Statues," a small boy is sitting on a wall outside a casino with his mother. Her boyfriend is inside at the card table. This is based on a true story. The last time I visited Las Vegas for a bookstore event, I stayed with friends—performers from a Las Vegas Cirque du Soleil show. Over dinner, one of their friends mentioned how as he was leaving the casino after work, he witnessed the scene with the boy sitting on the wall. I felt very sad about the whole idea and, after dinner, wandered the streets in an attempt to grasp the feeling of alternating hope and despair that fills Las Vegas. Las Vegas is one of the only places I've ever visited where you can walk the streets in the middle of the night without ▶

being noticed because there are so many people—then take a very short cab ride into the desert and experience total, absolute isolation.

How Characters Get Their Names

The protagonist from "The City of Windy Trees" is a young man named George Frack. I found the name written on a label sewn into a jacket I bought from a man selling clothes out of a suitcase on the Upper West Side. The jacket was actually attached with a hanger to the wire fence of a basketball court. When I first saw the man, I wondered what he was doing selling clothes. I wondered how the jacket was attached to the fence. From a distance the jacket looked as though it were trapped in a giant spider's web—and that the owner of the jacket had escaped a ghastly fate by simply taking off his coat and walking away down West End Avenue. The man selling the jacket motioned at me to come over and try it on. So I did. Then an old woman passing said something like, "That really suits you." And I wondered whose jacket it really was or had been, and how I could so easily slip into their life— and how willing people are to give you another chance. So I bought it for seven dollars, and when I got

> ❝ I found the name [George Frack] written on a label sewn into a jacket I bought from a man selling clothes out of a suitcase on the Upper West Side. ❞

10

home, I noticed a name tag: George Frack.

I dream of a rural life and so try to spend some time at a humble cottage in the French countryside every summer. Last summer I was working on the story "Love Begins in Winter," and I couldn't think of an appropriate name for the male protagonist. On a shopping trip to Saumur (I really, really love French supermarkets), I drove past an old advertisement from the 1940s for Dubonnet (a wine-based aperitif), where the "Du" was covered by ivy. Someone in the car, still a little drunk from lunch, said "bonnet" out loud and laughed to himself. And I immediately thought: "Bruno Bonnet." It sounds beautiful and ridiculous at the same time, depending on whether it's spoken with a French or English accent, and I sort of like that.

The female protagonist in "Love Begins in Winter" is named after a girl I had a crush on when I was fifteen, so I was able to use those feelings—which I remember very clearly. However, I didn't think to use her name at the beginning: My agent didn't like the old name ▶

How to Find a Story *(continued)*

(Hazel) and remarked one day on the phone that is sounds too "witchy."

"How about something like Hannah?" he said, and I thought: "Hannah? God, how I loved her!"

A Final Note on Characters

I always meet interesting characters on my travels, and occasionally I make a lasting friend. However, I don't *use* people for stories, I *use* stories to express my feelings for people. ◠

What I Do When I'm Not Writing Books

DESIGN, CUT, SEW, AND FIT clothes for dolls with my daughter, whom I live with in New York City. See Fig. 1

Take photos with my daughter at every photo vending machine we pass. Fig. 2. was taken at Charles De Gaulle Airport in Paris, 2008.

Sit on benches and feed birds.

Read books because I love them, not because I think I should read them.

Fig. 1

Travel alone.

Listen to J. S. Bach.

Hang around airports.

Run.

Watch 1960s Italian and French films.

Cook grand suppers. Here are some things I make at least three times per week. When I find a story somewhere, I also try and take a recipe home so I know what my characters might be eating ▶

Fig. 2

for dinner as I write about them. Here are two recipes:

1. The Roman Diplomat's Salad (an easy dish Max makes for his Italian girlfriend in Rome). For this recipe, you'll need:

    Fresh spinach
    One ripe orange
    Pecorino Romano (cheese)
    Olive oil and balsamic vinegar

    Arrange the spinach in a crown on a large plate. Then peel the orange and take every last bit of skin from each segment. (If you're lazy, like me, you can buy mandarin segments in a can—though it won't taste as good.) Place the orange segments on top of the spinach about one inch apart. Then slice very thin the Pecorino Romano and lay sections (about the size and width of a razor blade) in between the orange segments. Then add oil and balsamic vinegar. I promise you will have great success with this salad.

2. Biff Rydberg (Lotta's favorite— she taught George how to cook

it in her play kitchen). For this recipe you will need:

Six to eight medium potatoes
Four tablespoons of butter
Two onions (the ones that make
  you cry)
One pound of beef tenderloin
Worcestershire sauce
Crème fraîche
Chopped parsley
Salt and pepper

Chop the potatoes into slices while gently melting the butter in a pan. Slip the potatoes in and cook slowly for a while—then crank the heat to crisp the outsides (yum yum!). Take them out and put them to one side—adding more butter to cook the onions (add the onions!) until soft. Then take the onions out and cook the beef with a few good shakes from the bottle of Worcestershire sauce. When the beef is cooked, put it on a plate beside the potatoes and the pile of onions. I add a dollop of crème fraîche, chopped parsley, and salt and pepper to the beef. I also like to eat toast with it. This dish will keep you warm while reading *Love Begins in Winter*. ▶

What I Do When I'm Not Writing Books
(continued)

I also like to eat ice-cream cones while writing. Sometimes my daughter will come home from school, see the box of cones sitting on the counter, and say, "How many of these have you eaten?"

Final Note

I think that if *you* were to write a story, it would be one of the most intimate acts you could ever undertake, simply because language outlives us.

One hundred years from now, in 2109, the great-great-great-great-great-great-great-great grandchildren you will never meet will be able to walk to school and think about your secrets.

Language allows us to reach out to people, to touch them with our innermost fears, hopes, disappointments, victories. To reach out to people we'll never meet.

It's the greatest legacy you could ever leave your children or your loved ones:

The history of how you felt.

These stories are the history of how I felt. ◡